Theaker's Quarterly Fiction #57

Edited by
Stephen Theaker
& John Greenwood

Theaker's Quarterly Fiction #57

Edited by
Stephen Theaker
& John Greenwood

Cover Artist

Howard Watts

Interior Art

John Greenwood

Contributors

Antonella Coriander
Douglas J. Ogurek
Howard Watts
Jacob Edwards
Rafe McGregor
Walt Brunston

Contents

CONTENTS
7

Editorial

Stephen Theaker

This Issue

Welcome to issue fifty-seven, a little bit late! My hobby is essentially the same as my job, albeit with different subject-matter, so when it's crunch time with my work that's what soaks up my time at the desk. And then November is of course when I write a novel – or at least try to. This year was a washout in that regard, unfortunately! Nevertheless, here it is at last, our *fifth* issue of the year, and I hope you'll really enjoy it!

The stories by Antonella Coriander and Walt Brunston are perhaps not their best, but Rafe McGregor's contribution is as brilliant as you'd expect from reading his previous work in the magazine (nb. he asks readers to bear in mind that the dated attitudes of the characters are *not* those of the author), and we also have a brand new story from Howard Watts. What's more, Rolnikov, for many years nothing but my online handle, is restored to his glory in "Nold", the beginning of a epic saga originally promised *last century* in the "folderback" edition of *Professor Challenger in Space*!

Issue fifty-eight will be our unsplatterpunk edition, edited by our US film correspondent Douglas Ogurek, so before he takes charge I'll use this opportunity to mention a few interesting things we'll be doing next year.

The TQF Awards

First: the TQF awards! For the last four years, and a couple of other years a bit further back, I ran the British Fantasy Awards, which was absolutely fascinating and thoroughly enjoyable. I stepped down in September, because their current system took up a disproportionate and unsustainable amount of my time. Fourteen separate awards, all juried, require a lot of administration! (I gave a full year's notice, so it wasn't as if anyone was left in the lurch.)

Anyway, to innoculate myself against re-volunteering, and also to give myself the chance to experiment in a way that was never possible with the BFAs, I have decided to introduce our own TQF awards. These will let me have much of the fun of running the BFAs, with little of the hard work! The only items eligible will be those that have been reviewed in our pages, and the only categories will be those that have appeared in the Quarterly Review, plus three about our magazine: best story, cover and issue. Voting will be open to everyone, and my plan at the moment is to let people vote for as many items in each category as they like.

One interesting aspect of our awards will be that while nominations for most awards are restricted to items published during the previous year, older material will be eligible for ours, since we often review older books that we happen to have read. Could produce some interesting results!

We'll probably kick things off in January.

Corrupt Reviews for Cash

Second: Corrupt Reviews for Cash! This is my moneyraising venture for next year's Comic Relief. I will be taking your dirty backhanders to review your books on Red Nose Day. Five pounds and a review is yours! We won't even need to read the book; I am such a perspicacious reviewer that a book cover and a description will be more than enough for me to see to its very heart!

The reviews will probably appear on a separate Corrupt Reviews for Cash blog that we've set up. We hope that they will raise money, a chuckle or two, and awareness of the scourge of paid reviews, helping people to spot the telltale signs of corruption!

We'll be reviewing the books in order of donation to Comic Relief via our JustGiving page, so get on over there and book your slot: www.justgiving.com/fundraising/corrupt-reviews-for-cash.

A New Book

Third: a forthcoming book! We swore off publishing any new books by other people, because our previous titles had been so unsuccessful (the fault being entirely mine), but we have been persuaded to give it one last go, with a fantastic new collection of stories by one of our earliest contributors, Rafe McGregor. We are aiming for a March publication date. Keep an eye out for news next year.

Contributor News

Douglas J. Ogurek's "Torrentious Pyreel's Defeat," an

unsplatterpunk tale about a violent supernatural torturer/golfer who enlists the story's protagonist to exact revenge, featured in *HelloHorror*, and his "The Dink, the Donk, and the Poo Pile" appears in issue 101 ("Schlaraffenland") of *Danse Macabre*, a magazine of the magical and the absurd. See www.hellohorror.com and www.dansemacabremagazine.com.

Stephen Theaker's reviews, interviews and articles have appeared in Interzone, Black Static, Prism and the BFS Journal, as well as clogging up our pages. He shares his home with three slightly smaller Theakers, no longer runs the British Fantasy Awards, and works in legal and medical publishing.

The Elder Secret's Lair

Ms. found under a stone in the ruins of Zimbabwe during the Caton-Thompson Survey, 1929

Rafe McGregor

I

Much to the disappointment of my father and eldest brother, I turned down a commission in the Coldstream Guards for the Bechuanaland Border Police, but I had no regrets. Instead of two years of parading up and down Constitution Hill, I'd been thrown headlong into the mystery, adventure, and excitement of the Dark Continent. When war broke out with the Matabele six weeks ago, I was despatched to Rhodesia. Major Forbes had taken his flying column north to hunt King Lobengula and his missing *impis*; I'd been given command of the dozen fastest riders and sent east, on the trail of the king's grandmother. Sophonisba was reputed to have been born in the eighteenth century, the daughter of the great Zwide of the Ndwandwe people, and to possess great powers as a *sangoma* and an *inyanga*. The combination of her

skills in the arts of both divination and healing made
her a powerful witch doctor, with sufficient influence
to prolong the war if she so desired. Lobengula had
given her a guard of forty of his best warriors to escort
her to safety in Manicaland. My men and I followed,
covering just under two hundred miles in just over a
week and picking up her trail on the banks of the
Lundi River.

Two days ago – the 3rd December 1893 – I decided
to divert to Fort Victoria for fresh horses and we set off
at dawn next morning. My scout, Brocklehurst, found
the *spoor* again at midday and I ordered a break for
luncheon shortly after, when we discovered the
smouldering remains of Sophonisba's wagon. The
route she had selected climbed the spur upon which
the fabled ruins of Zimbabwe were built and the steep
slope was thick with shrubs, thorn bushes, and
spreading trees. There was no question we wouldn't
catch her, but the torrential rain of the last few days
had made the ground treacherous and I wanted my
men fresh in case her bodyguard put up a fight. Once
the sun passed its sweltering zenith we pushed on. We
crested the rise at five o'clock and I halted to take in
my first view of the ancient city.

The part of the stronghold still standing, an
elliptical enclosure about a hundred yards across, was
a quarter of a mile to the south-east of our position, in
a natural basin formed by the surrounding hills. A
high, bare *kopje* dominated the landscape to the north
and a valley cut through the granite half a mile to the
east, directly ahead of us. The *veldt* in front of the
ruins was flat, with trees scattered in the grass. There
were more ruins in the hills to the south, stones barely
visible through the tropical forest. Clouds brooded
overhead, but the day was still bright and we had an
hour and a half until sunset. I removed my hat, wiped
the sweat from my forehead with my sleeve, and

scanned the vista for movement. Brocklehurst was doing the same with his field glasses. Sergeant Mackenzie, who had accompanied me from Bechuanaland with Trooper Kinloch, brought his horse alongside mine.

"Is that the lost city, sir?"

"What's left of it, yes."

"Looks like a good place to hide."

I nodded. "Anything, Willie?"

Brocklehurst lowered his glasses. "No. The *spoor* leads straight down to the ruins. Either they've taken refuge there or they've pushed on out the other side. A mile in front of us, no more."

If it came to a fight, I wanted to do it before the sun set. My orders were to capture Sophonisba not kill her and anything could happen during a skirmish at night in the pouring rain. I put my hat back on and turned to face the company. Forbes had given me a bunch of rogues to lead, the scrapings of the southern African colonies, but tough fighting men every one. There were two Boers, Van der Heyl and De Vos; an American, Bax; and a half-breed Hottentot from Raaff's Rangers called Meikljohn. My other sergeant, Bain, was a Rhodesian policeman and had four of his men with him, Kirton, Nesbit, Nunn, and Pickman. Pickman was from Natal, carried a giant knife that was a cross between a D-Guard Bowie and a Swahili panga, and looked like he could use it.

"Straight down to the ruins. Sergeant Bain, peel off to the right with six men; the rest follow me. If we draw fire from the ruins, we'll dismount and form two skirmish lines. If we don't, we'll meet at the entrance and go in on foot. Regroup at the stand of mopane trees. Remember, Sophonisba has ten servants with her, but she'll be the oldest woman in the group. For God's sake don't shoot her by accident."

I looked at every man in turn. They all understood.

There was no need to say any more. I nodded to Bain, removed my rifle from its scabbard, and followed him down the slope. Although the grass remained flat from Sophonisba's flight, the descent was difficult. I had to be careful to keep my horse from going too fast because the ground was soft and scattered with rocks of all sizes. Weaving between trees and boulders, we nonetheless reached the floor of the basin quickly. The ruins were two hundred yards away and I was planning my route when I heard the multiple cracks of ragged rifle fire from the rear.

"Halt!" I shouted. Stopping in an ambush was precisely the opposite of what I would've been taught at Sandhurst, but the Matabele were notoriously poor shots. So far in the war their most effective weapon had proved the throwing *assegai*: their lack of training made their rifle fire ineffective and they hadn't succeeded in coming close enough to use the *iKlwa*, the deadly melee weapon designed by Shaka. I turned my horse. "Willie, how many?"

The rest of the men were also turning, reins in one hand and a rifle in the other. The sound of the shots echoed off the *kopje* to the north.

"They've circled behind us. There's about twenty – no, thirty!" He was watching the smoke from the muzzles.

Mackenzie tugged at my sleeve. "Sir, there's more – up there!"

I followed the line of his rifle and saw puffs of smoke rising from the *kopje*. It wasn't just the echo; there were men up there as well, the rest of the bodyguard.

"Sergeant Bain, take cover in the ruins and keep their heads down. Sergeant Mackenzie, follow me, we'll outflank the snipers on the *kopje*."

I followed Bain across the *veldt*. He peeled off to the right. I touched my horse's flanks, breaking into a canter. The rifle fire from the north had intensified and when I looked up again I saw considerably more smoke than before. There were at least thirty men up there, perhaps fifty. I glanced behind me and saw exactly what I wanted: a line of six riders, each man in his saddle, all keeping their distance from one another. Meanwhile Bain's men were out of sight, having proceeded around the south side of the ruins. Shots continued to crack and ring without coming any closer. When I reached the middle of the triangle made by the *kopje*, valley mouth, and great enclosure, I reined back, letting Mackenzie lead the men to the valley – from where we would begin our assault on the *kopje*. The entrance to the ruins was now two hundred and fifty yards away. I couldn't see any of Bain's men, who should have been approaching from the other side. I drew my horse up as Brocklehurst flew past me.

A bullet buzzed close and I ducked involuntarily.

Bain emerged from the trees firing his rifle in the air, his cape suspended behind him. Nesbit was next and he also fired into the air. They were both shouting, but I couldn't hear what they were saying. Another bullet buzzed close. Someone on the *kopje* had my range and I couldn't afford to remain still any longer. I spurred my horse towards Bain and saw Pickman, Kirton, Bax, and Meikljohn, but not Nunn.

"Matabele – hundreds of them – coming from the south!"

Bain was right. On the slope to the south I could see the smoke of the Matabele rifles and the whites of their shields. Sophonisba's bodyguard had been reinforced. Bain and I reined in together.

I pointed with my rifle. "The valley, that's our way out – make sure Mackenzie knows! Where's Nunn?"

Bain shook his head, applied his spurs, and shouted to the rest of his men: "The valley – follow me to the valley!"

I turned my horse around and felt the breath of another bullet. Sophonisba would have to wait. We were surrounded on three sides. It was time to save our souls. I dug my heels into my horse and immediately heard an unexpected sound – the low, loud roar of a mass of Matabele warriors on the charge. The war-cry was coming from the front, not the rear... seconds later, all of my men were galloping from the mouth of the valley, Brocklehurst in the lead.

"Five hundred warriors – they were waiting in the valley!"

I was surrounded on four sides. The trap had been sprung and the jaws were closing.

"The ruins – we'll make a stand in the ruins!"

I had no idea if the warriors from the south would reach the ruins before us, but they hadn't emerged from the dense foliage of the hill yet, so we had a chance. I turned my horse once again as my men raced for safety. Bax, the American, was last and we fell in step.

"My guess is four hundred on the ridge." He pointed south.

If he was right that made for a thousand-odd Matabele against my force of thirteen – no, twelve.

Bax's horse collapsed underneath him.

I dragged on my horse's reins yet again. I felt her shudder and stagger. She leaped forward screaming in agony, caught her front legs on a low stone wall, and tumbled over, hurling me into the air.

II

I hit the ground feet-first, crashed into a thin tree trunk and bounced off, losing my grip on my Martini-Henry. I sat on my rump for a couple of seconds, shook some sense into my head, and retrieved the rifle.

Bullets were flying thick and fast, both from above, on the *kopje*, and below, from the valley as the Matabele advanced. My horse was lying on her left side, panting, sweating, and bleeding. She'd been shot at least once and broken one of her forelegs. I whispered to her as I placed the barrel of my rifle behind her eye, then gave her the lead gift. I reloaded. Through the trees and scrub I could see dozens of dark figures: the brown, black, and white of flesh, ostrich-feather headgear, and cowhide shields. The closest were two hundred yards away and I was half that from the great enclosure. Bax was on his knees, firing rapidly.

"Bax, come on! I'll cover you."

He fired, reloaded, and staggered to his feet. Using the butt of his rifle, he hobbled towards me.

I lowered my rifle and ran to him. The Matabele were closing fast.

I was a few yards away when he lurched forward – a great patch of red on his chest – and fell on his face at my feet.

"Bax!"

I could see a bullet had entered high on his back. I stooped, pulled him over, and saw a huge hole near his heart from which blood was pouring. His eyes were dead. He was dead.

I dropped Bax and ran for the ruins. Threading my way through the scattered trees, over what was left of the outlying walls and rubble-filled striations, I approached the main entrance, which was nothing more than a breach where the wall had crumbled. Bain and Mackenzie had established a firing line and ten men were pouring rifle and revolver fire into the Matabele approaching from the south. Revolvers aside, each man was capable of firing one round every five seconds. Given the close range and the size of the bullet, this meant that if Bax was right about the numbers, my troop would have been able to kill or incapacitate well over a quarter of the southern horn of the Matabele assault in the first minute. There was a broken line of about two dozen bodies twenty-five yards away from my men and the ferocity of their fire had temporarily stalled the attack. The problem was that the northern horn was much larger and would soon be upon us.

I ran straight into the vine-hung ruins. The dry-stone structure was being strangled by the trees, with creepers, nettles, and thorns slowly squeezing the form from the granite brick. The horses had been sent inside, but there'd been no time to tether them, so I could only see a couple, off to the right. There was a bottleneck at the entrance, a series of walls of five feet or higher. To my left, a narrow passage between the outer wall, which must have been close to thirty feet high, and the inner wall, which was much lower. To my right, the inner wall disappeared after a few dozen yards, opening into the pen where the two horses waited, tense and skittish. I pushed on into the centre and saw a tower rising above the trees at the eastern end of the ellipsis. I couldn't see any windows or a doorway, but it was in a little enclosure of its own and would have to do.

I ran back to the rubble-strewn entrance. The front-runners from the northern horn had slowed down and the ranks were massing for an attack a hundred yards away. My men were still firing at the southern horn, although more sporadically as the targets were fewer. I tapped Bain on the shoulder.

"Hold here with four men. Mackenzie will cover you from the ruins. When I give the order take your men inside and set up a defence of the tower." He nodded. Mackenzie had already seen me. "Take four men, pull back to the entrance." I pointed north. "They're preparing to charge again."

An orderly retreat is one of the most difficult

military manoeuvres to perform, but my men behaved admirably. I joined Mackenzie's skirmish line in front of the breach and we began firing at the sea of bodies in the trees. I yelled for Bain to move and saw five men dart for the ruins. Nesbit was hit, stumbled, and was seized by Kirton and Meikljohn. I shouted to Mackenzie and Brocklehurst to cover the south – there was a roar as the charge from the north was launched. Bain and his men had made it.

"Pull back, into the ruins!"

Mackenzie moved first, setting up a position fifteen yards into the ruins, between two walls. I fired at the warriors racing towards us, now fifty yards away. Brocklehurst followed, then Van der Heyl and De Vos. I fired one more time, reloaded, and beat a hasty retreat. Kinloch fell down in front of me and I had to jump over him so I didn't trip. He'd been hit by an *assegai* flung from my left – the southern horn had taken heart at the sound of the northern horn and was also on the charge.

"Captain!"

I was caught in the frame of the breach and Mackenzie was shouting for me to get out the way. I knelt down next to Kinloch, raised my rifle, and fired. Over my head, the pitifully small volley from inside. I grabbed Kinloch and was about to drag him when a hail of throwing *assegais* struck. Two hit Kinloch and one took off my hat. I left him as a group of twenty warriors closed.

"The tower, make for the tower!"

I reloaded, dashing into the bottleneck. Van der Heyl had gone the wrong way, jumping over a wall to the right. I roared to him to follow me – saw Matabele pouring through the breach – and threw myself over a wall to the left. I hurdled one stone barricade and sprinted to the next, heading for the tower, thirty yards away. Twenty yards to my right, I saw De Vos

turn, fire, and fall as he was swamped by Matabele.
Mackenzie and Brocklehurst joined me. Bain and his
men had started firing from the walls in front of the
tower, picking off the warriors that followed us
through the granite maze. I glanced over my shoulder
to the left, saw the headring of an *nDoda* – senior
warrior – an arm's length away, and fired point-blank
into his chest.

Six other warriors used the line of the inner wall to
outflank us. Brocklehurst and Mackenzie stopped and
fired. A warrior closed on me, striking with his shield
and raising his *iKlwa*. I let the blow knock me off
balance, dropping my rifle and reaching for my holster
as I fell. I hit the ground, rolled to my right, and felt
the blade pass by my cheek. The warrior stamped on
my ribs and drew his *iKlwa* back for another strike, but
I had my Webley free and shot him in the face. I
scrabbled to my feet. Mackenzie was stabbed in the
thigh and staggered. I shot the warrior in the temple,
grabbed Mackenzie, and made for the tower.
Brocklehurst covered our flight, firing and reloading
with superhuman speed.

I reached Bain and his men, my revolver in my right
hand and Mackenzie's rifle in my left, dragging him
with me. Bain was kneeling on top of a wide stretch of
wall; Pickman, Kirton, and Meikljohn had taken up
positions behind the inner wall, and the wounded
Nesbit was propped on a pile of stone. Brocklehurst
joined Bain on the rampart, but Mackenzie and I
simply collapsed where we were and started shooting.
Dozens of Matabele swarmed towards us, holding
their shields up for protection and screaming their
fearsome war-cry.

In the next thirty seconds we dropped fifty of them.

Bullet after relentless bullet brought the charge to a
bloody halt. A huge *inDuna* – chieftain – whose
headdress and cape made a Goliath of him, came the

closest to our fragmented line, falling five yards in front of me. When I'd emptied my revolver, I removed Mackenzie's from his holster and made each shot count. The warriors hesitated, their roar faltered, and Bain bellowed to us to keep firing. Brocklehurst, as ever with his wits about him, threw me his revolver and another six warriors fell, caught in the open ground between the inner wall and the beginning of the disorderly labyrinth. By the time a minute had passed, the thirty-yard stretch was littered with seventy-odd bodies. Some were still, some crawling, but most writhing in the agony of their death throes.

I pulled Mackenzie up and assisted him to cover behind the inner wall. I threw Brocklehurst's revolver back to him and asked if anyone had any spare rounds for mine. No one did so Kirton passed me his and Nesbit's revolvers. Nesbit was in a bad way, barely conscious, a bullet lodged somewhere in his stomach. I considered running back to retrieve my rifle, but decided it was too dangerous, with sporadic shots still coming from behind the walls to the west. Some of the men took hasty drinks from their canteens and I used the respite to inspect the tower.

It was a strange structure, situated in the space between the inner and outer wall and rising higher than both. At this point the gap between the two walls was large and the tower must have been about twenty feet in diameter at its base and about thirty-five feet high. There were no entrances or apertures and it looked as if it were solid. I'd hoped we'd be able to use it as a redoubt, but that was impossible. Nonetheless, we had the outer wall at our back, two narrow approaches between the inner and outer walls to our left and right, and the open ground in front. With twenty men, I could've held the position for some time. I had seven, two of them wounded, one badly. To make matters worse, the sun was very low and sunset

would soon be upon us. Pickman assisted me with
Nesbit. We leaned him against the tower to take the
stress off his stomach. I took his rifle and gave him the
two revolvers. Bain and Brocklehurst were covering the
northern approach so I joined Meikljohn to cover the
southern. My only hope was that the moon would be
bright, but the clouds were stacking high, brooding
heavily after the heat of the day.

The sniping from the *kopje* had long ceased for fear
of the Matabele hitting their own. The fire from within
the ruins petered out as Bain and Brocklehurst picked
off any warrior rash enough to raise his head above the
stone. Soon, neither man could spy any unwounded
from their vantage point. Though we could hear the
movement of hundreds of men from beyond the walls,
the Matabele seemed to have retired from the ruins *en
masse*. The sun sank lower and I checked my watch:
quarter to six. When I looked up again, I realised that
a hush had descended over the battlefield. The
warriors we couldn't see were no longer moving and
the only human noises were the quiet groans and
muffled cries of still-breathing bodies on the open
ground.

From the outside the ruins, a high-pitched trilling
cut through the sounds of the *veldt*, a howling
ululation that chilled me to the bone.

Sophonisba had joined us.

III

I spoke loudly, so that all seven men could hear me
above Sophonisba's wicked wailing. "Gentlemen, it
seems that the time has come to either sell our lives
dearly or attempt to escape. I shall remain with
Sergeant Mackenzie and Trooper Nesbit, but there is
no dishonour in making a break for it. I'm certain that

a few of our horses are still in the enclosure. If we are not completely surrounded an escape may be effected to the west." The chances were slim, but to remain was certain death. "You can each let me know your decision in person." For myself, I regretted nothing. I was content to die in this ancient, eldritch place surrounded by the stout of heart alive and dead, black and white. I had no desire to exchange my short life of incident and exploit for a long, dull life of gradual descent into decrepitude and dotage. I had come to the Dark Continent seeking adventure; I could hardly complain that I'd found it. I moved along the inner wall, shaking hands with each man. They all decided to stay. We would make a final stand together. I was disappointed that I would not be able to commit the bravery of my men to record for the benefit of their families, but their corpses – and those of the enemy – would tell their own tale.

Twenty minutes later, Sophonisba's railing was embellished by her entourage and the ululation reached deafening proportions, echoing off the *kopje*. The sound intensified as the sun plunged towards the edge of the earth and I couldn't help imagining that the witch doctor and her servants were banishing the light from the sky – or raising the darkness from the nether-world. Once again, there was no need for orders. No need for any words whatsoever. We all knew what was going to happen and we all knew that the only thing we could do was take as many of the Matabele with us as possible. A determined rush, as Sophonisba's tender ministrations were no doubt intended to inspire, would reach us in well under a minute, no matter how many we managed to kill.

Another twenty minutes passed and then the ululating was joined by a loud, rhythmic thudding. The warriors were stamping the *veldt* with their feet, hundreds hitting the earth in perfect unison. I saw that Nesbit's head had fallen forward and I knelt down next to him. He was still breathing, but had lost consciousness. If he was lucky, he'd be killed in his sleep. I removed the two revolvers from his side, put one in my holster and returned the other to Kirton. Then I resumed my place next to Meikljohn, who was smoking a cigarette as casually as if he'd been sitting in the Café Royal.

Ten minutes later, the ululation and the thudding were reinforced by a third sound, the rapid beating of *iKlwa* hafts against shields. It was not long now. I checked my watch again – merely habit as I knew I'd already written my last report. Twenty-five to seven, a few minutes of sunshine before twilight took hold. I looked at the tower and wondered at its purpose once more. Was there something imprisoned inside or buried beneath? Was it monument or merely decorative? A fertility symbol for the performance of rites? I had hoped for a bastion to defend, but the granite was against us, a beacon to guide our foes. I snapped my watch shut, there was a flash of lightning, and the heavens opened.

The ululation reached an impossible crescendo.

The Matabele roared and charged into the ruins.

Dozens and then hundreds of dark figures darted amongst the stones, hurling themselves at us, baying for our blood in their frenzy. There was no rifle fire from them – they were going to kill us the traditional way, the blade into the belly slicing the intestines and drawing them out with the distinctive sound that gave the stabbing spear its name. I lost track of everything except my targets and Meikljohn next to me. We worked in splendid harmony: aim, fire, eject, load, close... aim, fire, eject, load, close... aim, fire, eject, load, close... four, five, six, seven...

I fired at an *iJaha* – junior warrior – a few feet away and jumped down from the inner wall, retreating to a small space between the tower, the outer wall, and the twin trunks of a mopane tree. Meikljohn was on my left shoulder and we both fired again as three warriors appeared on top of the wall. Two were thrown back, but the third jumped down and stabbed Meikljohn in the arm. I dropped my rifle, drew my revolver, and shot the *iJaha* in the back. I looked up to fire at two more warriors. Meikljohn appeared at my right and dispatched a third. Through the rain I could see Pickman carving his way through flesh and hide with his great knife.

A group of warriors emerged from the gloom between the tower and the outer wall. Meikljohn and I fired, but they were too close for more than one shot and the weight of their rush knocked us back. I tripped over the *iJaha* who had stabbed Meikljohn, flailed in the air for a second, and fell backwards. My head hit something hard. I lost consciousness.

IV

I do not know how long I slumbered. It may have been a few seconds or a few minutes. When I came to, I was wedged between the *iJaha*, the roots of the mopane tree, and Meikljohn – who lay on top of me, his back pressing against my chest and his shoulders covering my head. The revolver was still in my right hand; my left was trapped under the warrior. Matabele cries of triumph tore through the sound of the rain battering the earth. When I whispered to Meikljohn he neither replied nor moved. I knew what was coming next. Once all of my men were dead or – like me – incapacitated, the warriors who had killed them would conduct the ritual of *hlomuhla*. Although the Matabele were a martial tribe that had carved a bloody path across Natal, the Transvaal, and Rhodesia, the man who took a life was nonetheless tainted. As such, he would slit the stomach of the man he had killed. This allowed the vanquished man's spirit to escape to freedom and prevented it from haunting the victor. After freeing the spirit, the warrior would take an item of clothing from the dead man and wear it in order to cleanse himself of his deed.

Someone would shortly be back to disembowel poor Meikljohn. When they did, they would take his tunic from him and find my body below. The warrior would either think I was dead and disembowel me or realise I was alive and stab me to death. There was no escape. I couldn't remember how many bullets I had left in the Webley, but I thought it might be three. I would try to make each one count.

I heard the *iKlwa* sound and guessed it was Pickman's belly being ripped open. Then voices close by. I couldn't see anything with Meikljohn's neck flattening my nose. I heard at least two warriors approach. I was still learning the native language and couldn't understand what they said. I heard – and felt – the *iKlwa* slice across Meikljohn from left to right. He didn't flinch; at least the poor man was dead. I held my breath, gripped my revolver tightly, and thumbed back the hammer. There was more talking as Meikljohn was pulled up. I saw a dark figure loom above me and the branches of the tree above him, but the rain obscured any further detail. Meikljohn was half-way off me when an ululation pierced the beating of the rain. The warrior stopped for a moment, let Meikljohn fall back on top of me, grabbed his hat, and disappeared. I exhaled, eased the hammer of my revolver back down, and relaxed. The ululation grew louder and higher-pitched and this time it seemed to draw the water from the clouds, draining them dry. The howling and the hammering of the rain faded into the background as I lost consciousness once more.

V

Again, I had no idea how long I slumbered, although this time I had a feeling it was more a case of hours than minutes. The first thing I noticed was the brightness: the rain had stopped and the clouds cleared, leaving the ruins bathed in moonlight. The second thing I noticed was a wild shrieking coming from somewhere nearby. I thought it might be hyenas calling their packs to come and feed from the scores of carcasses our skirmish had provided. I was reassured by the feel of my revolver in my right hand and realised there was no *iJaha* trapping my left arm. A thin mist was rising from the ground and I could see very little from my supine state despite the half-light. The shrill screaming continued, but I heard no sounds of humanity and decided to take stock of my situation. I gently dragged Meikljohn's corpse from my chest and wriggled away from him. I rose to a crouch, my knees aching with the effort, and leaned against the mopane tree. I was close enough to the bodies of Pickman and Nesbit to make out their features through the swirling haze. Bain's body was prostrate on the raised rampart and Brocklehurst was wedged between rampart and tower. Mackenzie's cadaver was right behind me and Kirton's behind him. All six men had been disembowelled like Meikljohn and four had been stripped of their tunics. I swallowed hard, mouth dry and lips cracked, breathing in the thick, metallic odour of blood. I reached for my watch and found it had been smashed in the struggle.

I cocked the Webley again in case a curious hyena should appear from the gap in the inner wall and stood up slowly, holding the stone for support. I peered over the granite. The open ground was devoid of corpses, except for De Vos, whose body lay bare-chested in the mist precisely where he had fallen during our desperate dash for safety. The Matabele did not usually interfere with their own dead in any way other than to place a shield over a warrior who had died in battle. In this respect, they are far more enlightened than us, attaching no importance to the mortal remains of departed spirits, leaving them for the jackals and vultures. I wasn't sure if it was because I was standing or because the volume had increased, but the shrieking seemed louder. I stood completely still, trying to make out what it was, where it was coming from, and if it was moving towards me. As I listened, I realised the sound was more like a chant than a scream and was emanating from the entrance to the enclosure. I squinted into the night, but couldn't discern anything against the silhouette of the outer wall.

Suddenly, I caught movement amongst the creeper-covered granite. The chanting – for that's what it was – was coming closer.

I aimed the Webley at the figure that appeared in the moonlight, resting my forearm on the wall.

Sophonisba.

She stopped a few feet from De Vos's corpse, facing the tower, that sinister stone cone turned leprous in the luminescence, unwindowed and malign. She was small and slight, completely bald, and clearly closer to her century than half-century. She wore a simple hide dress under a heavy, hairy black cloak. I could hear the words she was chanting.

"...ä! Iä! Shub-niggurath! Ya-R'lyeh! N'gagi n'bulu bwana n'lolo! Mdobi ngaphandle, bayete! ä! Iä! Shub-niggurath! Ya-R'lyeh! N'gagi n'bulu bwana n'lolo! Mdobi ngaphandle, bayete! ä! Iä! Shub-niggurath! Ya-R'lyeh! N'gagi n'bulu bwana n'lolo! Mdobi ngaphandle, bayete..."

I understood some of them. *Bwana* is the native

word for "master", *bayete* the form of praise reserved
for a king. *Mdobi ngaphandle* meant something like
"fisherman from outside" – or perhaps it was "fisher
from outside". It made no sense because the Matabele
are a warrior people who do not hold herders,
fishermen, or farmers in high esteem.

"...ä! Iä! Shub-niggurath! Ya-R'lyeh! N'gagi n'bulu
bwana n'lolo..."

I relaxed a little. Sophonisba repeated the same
words over and over again, her intonation steady, her
volume unvaried. Minutes passed and I remembered
how thirsty I was. My own canteen was lost. I looked
at the seven bodies sprawled around me and
considered searching them, but I didn't want to lose
sight of Sophonisba, even for a moment. I turned back
to her and saw the mist rising into the moonbeams,
tendrils twisting playfully and then evaporating. The
haze became thicker, forming a gently rolling grey
carpet above the grass. Sophonisba had wrung the
water from the clouds, now she was extracting it from
the earth. It reached her knees, hiding her legs, and
rose halfway up my boots.

"...*Mdobi ngaphandle, bayete!*"

The chant stopped abruptly.

Sophonisba unfastened her cloak, twirled it like a
matador's cape, and let it fall into the fog at her feet.
Her hands fell to her sides, she closed her eyes and
started to sway. While I watched her I noticed a
movement of the mist near De Vos's body, rising on a
zephyr. Sophonisba continued to rock as if blown by a
breeze. I was waiting for her to lose her balance when I
noticed another movement in the mist, a ripple that
seemed to have substance, undulating across the
surface in the direction of the tower. At first it looked
like a mottled cloak, then a single scaly hose. I
followed the line of its progress with my revolver. The
shadow reached the foot of the wall upon which Bain's

body lay and then... the blood turned to ice in my veins.

I saw what looked like a giant spotted python slither up the stone. The snake must have been at least as long as a man at full stretch and at least as thick as a woman's waist. I had seen every type of python, mamba, and cobra native to southern Africa, but never a creature covered in hair. The beast coiled itself around Bain's legs and buried what must have been its head in his open belly.

Cold sweat trickled down my neck. My revolver would not be enough. If I rummaged for a rifle in the fog, I'd drawn attention to myself. The serpent was only twenty feet away. While I wavered in indecision, it detached itself from Bain and slid down the wall to where Brocklehurst lay, disappearing from view. I fought against my fear and forced myself to move, stepping slowly backwards, first over Mielkljohn's body and then Kirton's. There was another mopane tree a few feet to the south. I picked up Kirton's Martini-Henry, moving as quietly as possible, and pressed my back to the knotty bough of the tree. The breech of the rifle was empty, but I didn't dare load. Instead, I just clasped it tightly and hoped my nerve wouldn't fail.

The mist was up to my knees now, thick and opaque. I could see my own feet and Kirton's corpse in front, but little else. I heard a rustle as the serpent made its way to Nesbit, followed by a repulsive sucking when it found him. The process was repeated for Pickman. A shadow enveloped the place where Mackenzie's remains lay. Meikljohn would be next, then Kirton, then me. The sucking ceased. Silence. I beheld an inhuman shape... half-seen, half-guessed, half-solid, and half ether-spawned.

A face appeared in the mist and buried itself in Meikljohn's guts.

I retrieved a fresh cartridge from my ammunition pouch, loaded, and made ready to fire.

The wind picked up from the east, blowing clouds of fog towards me and obscuring my view of Kirton's corpse. The sucking again. I aimed into the haze. The sucking stopped, a shadow moved. The gust dispersed the mist covering Kirton.

In the moonlight, I saw a naked woman crouched over his stomach.

Slowly, she raised her head to look at me, blood dripping from her chin. Her long, lustrous jet-black hair was braided in ropes and strands that flowed down her back and onto Kirton's legs. Her complexion was a deep olive, like old ivory, with regular features and large, dark eyes. She stared right through me. I remembered a rhyme I had heard in Bechuanaland.

It is thus that the shadow grows mighty and whole,
As it feeds on the body and sucks at the soul.

The snake-woman rose to her feet. I trembled at the sight, the barrel of the rifle shaking unsteadily. She was about twenty years old, of medium height and slim build. She drew her hair around her like a writhing, wriggling cloak, concealing her form from me. She tiptoed over the carcass, her gait as graceful as a leopard. My quivering gave way to paralysis.

It is thus that the shadow grows mighty and whole,
As it feeds on the body and sucks at the soul.

She swept towards me. I tried to move the rifle and squeeze the trigger, but my muscles were leaden. I couldn't move. I couldn't breathe. Her mazing, piercing eyes were crimson in the yellow light. I was transfixed by her gaze, frozen with fear.

It is thus that the shadow grows mighty and whole,
As it feeds on the body and sucks at the soul.

As she brushed past me, a tendril of black braid tugged at the muzzle of the Martini-Henry. Something bristly landed on my right shoulder and curled around my throat. I found the use of my muscles again, screamed, and fired at the tower. The vine slid across my chest, swaying from a branch above. I spun around to defend myself... eject, load, aim...

Of the snake-woman, there was no sign.

Of Sophonisba, there was no sign.

VI

The sun has been up for an hour. I have been writing in my notebook all night, stopping only to sharpen my pencil. The Matabele removed the bodies of all their warriors from the ruins, leaving only those of my men inside. This must have happened during my second, prolonged, period of unconsciousness. The vampire-woman feasted on the flesh of all ten, draining the blood from their pale bodies to leave bleached corpses for the scavengers of earth and sky.

Who is she? What is her secret? Why did she spare me?

I do not know. I do know that she is the most intriguing and exquisite creature I have ever seen, a magnificent combination of beauty and beast. She inspires a simultaneous desire and dread neither of which I have experienced in a life full of event and interest. I have not slept since I saw her. I fear to dream for my unfettered imagination will betray either hot lust or cold terror and I know not which is worse.

I owe it to the brave men whose mortal remains lie about me to leave some record of their courage and of what passed here. I have tried to turn the strange sequence of events into a tale worthy of their deeds, but I have not stretched the truth at all, not dishonoured their memory with falsehood. If someone should find this notebook, I beg they will let the families of my men know that, as the Matabele say, *they fell like stones – each man in his place*. My place is not with them. I have one last adventure before me, the like of which I never thought to see.

Is she Haggard's Ayesha? The Queen of Sheba? An incarnation of Isis?

I do not know, but I am going to find out. I am going to find out why she spared me. I am going to discover her secret. I know not where she has gone, but Sophonisba will be continuing east, into the heart of Manicaland. I have Kinloch's horse, weapons and provisions to last as long as I need. I will seek Sophonisba. She shall tell me where to go. Then I will find my place, at the side of the Great White Queen.

CAPT. H.J. FLETCHER
BECHUANALAND BORDER POLICE

Rafe McGregor is the author of The Value of Literature, The Architect of Murder, five collections of short fiction, and over one hundred magazine articles, journal papers, and review essays. He lectures at the University of York and can be found online at https://twitter.com/rafemcgregor.

Nold

Stephen Theaker

Fight!

Pelney wondered if he would ever get to finish eating his strapple. It was just like Rolnikov to get into a fight at a time like this: just after Pelney had taken his first bite of the long green juicy fruit, but before he had taken a second, meaning that the whole thing would go brown if he didn't get back to it within a few minutes.

Pelney did consider, of course, the notion of continuing to eat his strapple while Rolnikov got on with his life-or-death battle. It would have seemed rude, though, even insouciant, so he held it, slowly browning, in one hand while the other hand shaded his eyes from this planet's twin suns.

"You're a fool to come here, Rolnikov!" shouted the fellow with whom he was fighting, a tall brutish man with a series of ragged tufts for hair. His eyes burned with hatred, his lips snarled with anger, and his fists lashed out with careless fury.

Such types often presumed that Rolnikov would be a pushover, since he rarely let the depths of his aggression show in anything more overt than a hard stare, *á la* Paddington. They often came to rue that presumption, usually about three quarters of the way into the fights.

This fight, Pelney judged, was one third of the way

through. They had passed the point at which tufty had realised this would not be a one-punch knockout, but not yet the point at which he would realise he could not win at all. It would be easy to tell when that point was reached, because he would be likely to resort to ever more desperate measures.

Pelney had seen one daft fellow take off his own socks and throw them at Rolnikov in a feeble last-ditch attempt to save himself. It had worked, up to a point. Rolnikov had let the man live, albeit with the socks sewn into his cheeks.

This guy with the tufts seemed to be wearing no socks. His feet were bare and calloused: he looked like nothing so much as a giant tufty halfling. In his hand there was now a knife.

Rolnikov had not taken his dread sword from the scabbard upon his back. He didn't need it for a street fight like this.

The giant halfling swung at Rolnikov with his left fist, while his right followed up with the knife.

Rolnikov dodged one, and twisted the other so that

"Pelney was awestruck by the beast that had disturbed his rest."
Illustration: John Greenwood

the knife fell to the ground. He kicked it away, making the ring of onlookers scatter.

Some were taking and making bets upon the fight; about half of these now had increasingly sullen faces. Others looked ready to step into the fight; on which side Pelney couldn't have said. Rolnikov had many enemies. The other guy couldn't have had many friends. He didn't look the sociable type.

Pelney was. He didn't want to be here, watching his best friend fight an aggressive stranger on the streets of a far-off world. He wanted to be back on Melrune, riding a five-eyed trondle through a grassy plain while playing on his pianolele to beautiful travellers riding in a charabanc.

He had been in that situation only a few weeks earlier, and his songs had been going down very well with one sweet-faced lady in particular. But it was not to be. That night the summons had come from the Orbiting Princess, and after escorting the charabanc safely to its destination Pelney and Rolnikov were on their way here, on an urgent mission of peace.

"Come on, Rolnikov," said Pelney under his breath. "We have a meeting to get to!"

He kept it under his breath because he was still not sure just how far his friend could be pushed. After all, Pelney called him a friend, and had done for many years, but would Rolnikov have called him a friend in return? He did not know. He hoped so. But he wasn't going to take any chances.

If it weren't for the imminent meeting, Pelney suspected this fight would already have been over. As Rolnikov jabbed his straightened fingers into first the ruffian's neck, and then into his ribcage, it was clear this was nothing but a game to him, a pastime, a bagatelle on the grand road of life.

Others had come to the same conclusion. Pelney

could see that the guy was about to do something
stupid.

"Don't do anything stupid!" he shouted, in hopes of
being helpful. "You'll only get yourself hurt worse.
Stick out your chin, take the punch, and lie down for a
nice nap, there's a good chap!"

The ruffian showed no sign of thinking this a good
suggestion. Even as a blow from Rolnikov caught him
in the small of the back he was reaching down to his
belt.

"The old belt as a whip trick!" laughed Pelney.
"We've seen them all, you know, ten times over!"

"Shut up," said a one-eyed man standing next to
Pelney, leaning on a cane. "You're spoiling the fight."

"This isn't a fight," said Pelney, shaking his head.
"Not really. It's a workout, mere exercise. My friend
here is working out the kinks after many weeks of
travel."

The one-eyed man waved his cane in Pelney's face.
"You'll shut your mouth or I'll smash every tooth in
your head."

Pelney looked the man up and down and decided
that despite his missing eye and need for a cane he was
probably capable of carrying out the threat.

Pelney gave him a nod, and said nothing.

At least for a moment.

As Rolnikov smacked his opponent upon the back
of the head with an outstretched arm, three of the
crowd made their move.

Pulling swords from their scabbards, they ran at
Rolnikov as one, even as his original opponent sank
unconscious to the ground.

"Hash seven seven nine!" shouted Pelney.

It was one of their prearranged codes. Pelney took
his responsibilities as squire very seriously, because
they were very serious responsibilities. And one of the
things he had done in recent years, to enhance his

performance of those duties, was to devise a series of alert codes with which he could advise Rolnikov of any threats and possible sources of advantage. Hash seven seven nine told Rolnikov how many men were attacking him, their positions, and what they were attacking him with.

Rolnikov gave the slightest of nods, then drew his sword in the smoothest of motions while pirouetting to meet the closest of them.

The attacker's sword clanged once against Rolnikov's black blade, which then slid around it, almost as if it were a snake, and found its way to the man's throat. His flesh opened, blossoming bright red fountains of gushing blood.

Rolnikov took a moment to let the blood cover him, the better to frighten the other two.

Rolnikov tried not to kill, because he knew it almost inevitably led to further trouble, vendettas, curses and the like, but there were situations in which it was unavoidable, and this was one of those.

He did not turn to face the other two attackers, but took three strides forward and cartwheeled three times through the crowd. It had already begun to scatter, in response to the spurting blood that threatened to soil their clothes. Now they began to run full-pelt away, dashing helter-skelter to escape the reach of this whirling dervish of a man, this spinning top of chaos, this tornado of swords and fists.

They need not fear. They are not his targets. Of the four men who attacked him, one lies dying, one rests in oblivion, one tries to stop his headlong rush, and one drops his sword and runs away. They have never seen anything like Rolnikov. Perhaps they heard stories, perhaps they didn't. Perhaps they chose this fight at random, perhaps they didn't. Whatever the case, they know now what they are dealing with, who they are dealing with, and it strikes fear into their hearts, terror into their marrow, shivers into their souls. For he is death itself in a tall, dark and handsome package, and it is their time to die.

He runs at the one left standing on the scene, raises an eyebrow as his black sword runs him through, from eyeball to ear. Rolnikov lifts the sword and flicks off the top of the man's head, almost casually, as an incidental amusement. He even laughs.

As the excitement which took us into the present tense fades, Pelney cautiously approached his friend and master, ready to perform his duties as squire.

"Stand down, Pelney," says Rolnikov. "I would wear this blood to our meeting. Let those who try to stop me from my purpose see how that tends to go."

"Certainly," replied Pelney. "The blood makes that perfectly clear. Do we need to worry about the guards I see approaching?"

He took a bite of his strapple. If they were to be arrested, it was now or never. It was quite brown, but that only made it sweeter.

"No," replied Rolnikov. "We have diplomatic immunity, of a kind. The kind that comes from being ready to kill any who should try to stop us."

"I'll have a word with them," said Pelney. "We don't want any more trouble. Or at least I don't."

He left Rolnikov staring at his dread black sword, holding it as if its strength was his, as if the blood upon it fed him, as if he couldn't bring himself to put it away.

The guards were relatively understanding after Pelney explained the situation, how they were here for the grand convocation of the uncivilised worlds, on behalf of the Orbiting Princess to represent the planet Melrune, and that these scoundrels had set upon them mere hours after their arrival upon Nold. The guards apologised for the inconvenience and directed Pelney towards the Great Hall of Knowing, where the convocation was on the point of commencement.

Pelney thanked them, and led Rolnikov in the right direction.

The Grand Hall of Knowing

The Grand Hall of Knowing was enough to make even Pelney gasp, and that was saying something because he had seen a *lot* in the course of his adventures with Rolnikov. It almost looked good enough to eat. Tall towers of spinning whisps stood at each corner, while at the centre loafed a golden globe, all the known knowledge of the universe scrolling across its surface, etched, erased and etched again by an army of infinitesimal humants.

"How do we get in?" asked Pelney, since there was no obvious entrance to the globe, or to the towers, and the size of the entire building was such that walking around its perimeter to discover a way in was less than appealing. He wanted to sit down and rest his little legs!

Rolnikov shrugged. "I don't know." He tried waving. "Ho there, let us in!"

There was no response, unsurprisingly, so Pelney looked around for clues.

Nold was not the kind of world that attracted much tourism. It was dangerous for dangerous people, never mind ordinary folk. Every street held a knifeman, every road a robber. Each avenue a bandit, each cul-de-sac a killer. Not the ideal place for diplomats to meet, but these weren't ideal diplomats.

No tourists, so no tourist information offices, no friendly faces, no signposts, or at least none that one would be wise to trust. They'd be as likely to lead you to your doom as to an attraction.

"They must have told the Orbiting Princess how to get in," said Pelney. "Could we call her on the talkoscanner and ask?"

Rolnikov shook his head. "It has limited power, and using it to call Melrune from so far away could exhaust it utterly."

"And she told you already, didn't she? You just forgot, and you don't want her to think you weren't listening?"

Rolnikov just grunted.

"I thought so," said Pelney with a grin so smug he might have got a clout if Rolnikov had been looking his way. "We'll have to figure it out then."

He walked closer to the globe. It was a perfect sphere, other than the imperfections upon its surface, and it rested lightly upon the ground, the tiniest of arcs in contact with the dirt of Nold. He presumed the four towers supported its weight, to create this impressive illusion, but could not be sure.

He came as close to it as was possible without bowing his head, and placed his hand upon its surface. The writing seemed to scatter from his hand, though that too was an illusion, the humants simply choosing not to write in that space while his hand was there.

He turned to face Rolnikov, who had quietly followed him. "They say you can ask the Grand Hall of Knowing anything you want, and it'll tell you, so long as your motives are pure and unselfish."

"I'd better do it then," said Rolnikov. "Since yours rarely are."

He placed his own hand upon the sphere's wall.

"Now ask!" urged Pelney. "With your mind... Or your voice... Whatever works."

"How does one enter the Great Hall of Knowing?" asked Rolnikov, his voice booming so loud one might have thought it the crack of a long-dormant volcano. "How do I get in?"

The tiny writers, products of a mysterious and mystical merging of humans and ants, enscribed the answer around his hand.

"That makes sense," said Rolnikov, and followed the instructions to the letter.

Three turns to the left, three turns to the right, a slap upon the top of his head, four clicks of the heels, a half-remembered joke, two thoughts about his mother, a wry half-smile, and the wall of the sphere broke out in a stairway.

"Say nothing," said Rolnikov, and Pelney did not. In fact he made a great show of pretending that he had not been watching any of it. He did not want Rolnikov to feel embarrassed.

They strode up the golden staircase together, and it gathered itself up behind them, like a paratrooper pulling in her chute. Nearby Noldians watched with greedy interest.

The two adventurers found themselves in a transparent lobby, a bubble from which they could see the Grand Hall of Knowing's interior, stretching away

"the malignant riverside statues of Grawmdall-Weel came to mind"
Illustration: John Greenwood

in every direction like a layabout with nothing better
to do.

It was clear that the blood which covered Rolnikov
would have little opportunity to make an impression.
He would soon be washed clean, because the interior
of the Grand Hall of Knowing was full of water.
Visitors could be seen swimming hither and thither,
consulting the inner walls or the giant thoughtfish
that carried the deep thoughts from one part of the
Hall to another. Others swam with the octopaedias
who wrapped their clever legs around them to collect
their information.

"Welcome to the Grand Hall of Knowing,
gentlemen!" said a jolly lady with what Pelney was
absolutely sure was an entirely genuine smile.

"Thank you," said Pelney. "It is a delight to be here."

Rolnikov nodded, feeling perhaps that the
conversation called for a small contribution on his
part. In normal circumstances he would have left it all
to Pelney, but he was conscious of his duties as a
representative of the Orbiting Princess. He did not
want her to be disappointed in him, as she had so very
many times before.

"Are you here for the summit?" she asked, shuffling
through a series of scrolls upon her desk.

"That's right," said Pelney, "the Great Convocation of
the Uncivilised Worlds."

"Well, well, I thought everyone was here except the
Orbiting Princess! Are you late additions to the guest
list?"

Pelney shook his head. " I am the squire Pelney and
this is Rolnikov, Mad Knight of Uttar Pradesh,
protector of Melrune. We are here on her behalf.
Events back home made it impossible for her to leave
Melrune at this time."

"You are fully accredited representatives,

empowered and able to engage in negotiations and commit to treaties?"

"We are," said Pelney. "In practice, I am likely to do the talking, while my friend and colleague here will deal with the empowerment."

"I see. Well, it all checks out. Let's get you both into your swimsuits, stow away your belongings (especially that big nasty sword), and get you through the waterlock and on your way to the Grand Convocation. I think they might have begun without you."

Once they were on their way, she went into a back room and chatted to a friend Orsula for a while about the weather, and if you think that only happened so that this story would pass the Bechdel test, you are absolutely wrong. They were going to have that chat whether this story was written or not, and regardless of whether you read it or not.

Pelney found the swimming quite difficult. He was only a little bit chubby, and he was in reasonably good health. His stamina was high, how could it not be with all the travelling the two of them did? But the water was thicker than usual, thick with information, knowledge pushing in from every side, and thick with things trying to get information from him, analysing the exposed areas of his skin, listening to the ticking of his brain. He slowly got used to it, but at first it was difficult, even oppressive.

If it bothered Rolnikov, Pelney couldn't tell. The tall warrior swam ever upwards, the wide sweep of his arms cleaving the water like a sword through an eyeball. The squire resisted the temptation to grab a foot and let himself be dragged up in the warrior's wake. He knew it wouldn't go down well with Rolnikov. He liked to keep his dignity, whenever possible, even when wearing a plastic breathing bubble upon his head.

At last they reached the top of the Great Hall of

Knowing, where a squad of squiddicles let them pass into the air bubble in which the meeting would take place, safe from prying eyes, and far from any maddening crowds. A platform floated upon the water, its surface an iridescent black, and if that combination should seem impossible it's not only that I haven't troubled myself to check the dictionary to see what iridescent means, it's also that the world of Nold is not like ours, not at all. Nold is a world of magic, not science, and its galaxy is one of future fantasy. If this is not yet entirely obvious, it shall become so in the fullness of this tale.

Upon the platform was a table, and around the table sat a number of serious-looking people, most of them irritated by these new arrivals.

"We've only just got the bloody table dry!" snarled a bearded man with a ponytail. "Why do they never listen? We've been doing this kind of thing for decades, and yet they never ask for our advice. What a stupid place for a Grand Convocation."

"We are very sorry," said Pelney, once the air bubble had been removed from his head by a pair of helpful sprawns. "We came as soon as we could. We represent Melrune."

"That pathetic little world?" said the greybeard. "I had conquered worlds like Melrune ten times over when I was your age. And does anyone remember it now. Of course not. No. No! Don't reply! If I want you to say anything else I will ask you a question!"

Pelney thought the man should count himself lucky that Rolnikov's helmet was still on. He turned to the head of the table, where sat an apparently frail woman with brown skin and white hair. She gave him a grim smile and nodded towards two empty seats at the table's far corner.

"Now we are all here at last," she said in a voice whose strength belied her age and size, "let us begin the Grand Convocation of the Uncivilised Worlds! We have much to discuss. First, let us introduce ourselves!"

The Grand Convocation

"Thank you for coming," said the grandmotherly lady once Rolnikov and Pelney had taken their seats. "We are all here for the same reason."

"To kill each other!" said the bearded man.

"Not this time," she said. "We should introduce ourselves. Our names may be the stuff of legends, but we have all been careful in the past to conceal our appearances from each other. I am Grandma Power. It is a foolish name, I know, but it was chosen by someone very dear to me and so I keep it. And of course it does reflect my methods. I control the planet Grandino and the space all around. I have killed ten men with my bare hands and enjoyed it less each time."

The bearded man looked at everyone else around the table, as if demanding that they speak. None did, so he harrumphed and took up the metaphorical baton. "I am Stentor Ploxton. The world of Chemicalia is mine. Our scientists are the finest in the galaxy and that lets us control the flow of the most desirable substances in the universe."

"Very impressive, I'm sure," said Grandma Power. "You, latecomers, introduce yourselves please."

Pelney looked at Rolnikov, who just stared back, not a single expression on his face. Pelney suspected that Rolnikov was rather hoping this situation would deteriorate to the point where he could justify killing every other person around the table, the consequences be darned.

"Me then," said Pelney, before taking a big gulp of

the drink so considerately provided by a sprawn. It tasted of bacon. "As I think we already said, this is Rolnikov and I am Pelney, his squire, herald and batman. We are here on behalf of the Orbiting Princess to represent the interests of Melrune."

"What is Melrune?" asked Stentor Ploxton with a sneer.

"It is large wild world with an unusual climate and a long-established population of humanoids and other beings. Technologically it is not very advanced, but we have other good qualities to compensate."

"I *know* about Melrune, you patronising little man," bellowed Ploxton. "And that's exactly the kind of response I expected from the representative of that world."

Pelney was nonplussed. He pursed his lips and shrugged. "Should I say sorry? I thought it was a sincere question so I gave you a sincere answer."

"It was clearly a rhetorical question! No answer was required, especially not at such tedious length!"

Pelney shook his head. "It is a common misconception that rhetorical questions don't need a reply. A simplification. The purpose of a rhetorical question is to make a point. Having made a point does not preclude rejoinders or disagreement with that point."

Smoke was coming out of Ploxton's ears by now. Quite literally. He was getting so hot and bothered, and the air was so moist, that he was literally steaming. He was on the point of doing something violent, thought Pelney, and if he had been there on his own he wouldn't have dared to provoke him in this way. The scientist was clearly possessed of a bad temper. That tended to be the way with interplanetary criminals.

"Why you little..."

Pelney interrupted him. "As I was saying before we

took a break to answer your question, this is Rolnikov, the man who slew the seven dragondines of Robuldinous Rabuldino, the fighter who defeated the king of the bramble mountain and his fifty thousand walking brains, the warrior who annihilated the seventeenth self-aware galaxy when it took to attacking its little sisters. Do you, Stentor Ploxton, want to see what happens if you attack his best friend?"

Ploxton was silent.

"That," said Pelney with a grand wave, "was a rhetorical question."

Rolnikov was very nearly smiling, thought Pelney. Anyone would have thought him almost happy for once. A rare thing indeed for Rolnikov, called the Doombringer, the Deathmonger, the Brainsplitter.

"Stop waving your Williams around," said Grandma Power. "We have more important things to do today than fight with each other. Indeed, we are here precisely to bring an end to that fighting. We could do so much more together than we could ever do at each other's throats. There are galaxies that could be ours, were we only to take a time out from fighting over this one."

"Why bring Melrune here, than?" demanded Stentor Ploxton. "The Orbiting Princess has been our enemy for many decades. I know she wants no part in this, and I could have told you that if anyone had bothered to ask."

"I take your point," said Grandma Power, "but I can answer it. None of us trust each other, but all of us trust Melrune. We may have no love for the Orbiting Princess and the infernal minions of Ibis (the Intergalactic Bureau of Investigation and Skulduggery), but she would never break a contract. If I can persuade each of you to join in the agreement I plan to put before you, Melrune will be witness to that agreement. If our treaty is announced by the Orbiting Princess, the galaxy will take it seriously."

"What's in it for her?" asked a thin woman in trousers, jacket, blouse and flat hat. Each hair on her head was a different colour.

Pelney answered. "Melrune wants peace in this galaxy, so far as possible. Should you become a serious threat to other galaxies, we will stand against you. But for now, a period of peaceful retrenchment would suit us as much as you."

This earned an approving nod from Grandma Power, which warmed the cockles of Pelney's heart even though he had spent an hour reading a list of her crimes without reaching the end of it.

"Please introduce yourself," said Grandma Power to the woman in the black suit.

"I am Zeddy Graves," she said, pulling her hair back into a ponytail, then immediately taking it out again. "I am here from Melodia. No one is in charge. All ideas are welcome."

"But only yours count," said Ploxton with a laugh.

"Not at all," said Zeddy Graves. "We are a co-operative planet of friends, working together to make it better for everyone. I am not their leader, I am just the person who happened to volunteer for this mission."

Everyone else knew not to volunteer, thought Pelney.

"We don't see ourselves as criminals. We simply want to share the benefits of our wonderful culture with everyone else."

At the point of a gun, thought Pelney. She was a music smuggler, the ringleader of a planetary gang who pushed mind-control music to the most vulnerable people they could find: teenagers. Once you controlled teenagers, you controlled the worlds that feared them.

A huge man with a shaved head covered in scars slammed his hand upon the table. "This meeting has gone on too long without me introducing myself."

"Go on then," said Grandma Power. "You are crucial to our plans, after all."

"I am Jack of Hands, the finest assassin in the galaxy. If you want someone dead, don't worry about it, I killed them already, all you need to do is pay me. And if you don't, I'll be killing you too."

"A remarkably efficent system," declared Pelney.

"Do you need anyone killed?" asked Jack of Hands, his face twisted in gruesome anticipation.

"Not at the moment, but if I ever do you'll be the chap I call. To be honest, and I usually am, my problem tends more often to be stopping people from getting killed. Do you have any experience in that area?"

Jack of Hands leaned forward further and stared intently at Pelney's face. "Do you want a knife in the eye?"

Pelney shook his head.

"Is that rhetorical enough for you?" laughed Stentor Ploxton with cruel enthusiasm.

"Jack of Hands represents the planet Dundoronum," interjected Grandma Power. "Home of a million murderers, cut-throats, assassins and stranglers."

"Don't forget the kittens," growled Jack of Hands.

"And lots of kittens," conceded Grandma Power. "But no cats, curiously."

"It's a conundrum," answered the assassin with a flash of his eyes.

A little lady with a head of curly hair filled the horrified silence. "This is not going to work. When I first heard about this organisation I thought it was dormant, and it seems to be dormant now. This Grand Convocation should be our shop window. Doing it in private like this will make everyone think it is over before it has begun."

"Thank you for your suggestions," said Grandma Power, "but there are obvious reasons why we must keep things quiet for now. Our people are out there in the universe fighting each other while we speak. None of us would want them distracted from their current activities. Should we come to the agreement I hope, we shall set down our weapons and plan for the future. A great future! But we are not yet ready. Please introduce yourself to our colleagues."

"I still think it looks like we're not doing anything. We need a shop window. Anyway, my name is Jonana Cassandrus. I am not currently a member of this organisation, but if there are signs of it coming to life perhaps that would make me want to join."

"And what do you do?" asked Pelney. At least as long as she was talking no one was threatening to kill him.

It was Grandma Power who answered, peering at him over her little round spectacles. "Jonana Cassandrus has been everywhere, and her people are everywhere. They prophesise the end, and are there to make sure it happens."

"The Monks of Death!" exclaimed Pelney, with such force it was necessary to use both an exclamation point and the word exclaimed.

"The Monks of Death," confirmed Grandma Power. "You can see why Jonana Cassandrus is so crucial to our cause."

The others around the table then introduced themselves too. They will be described later should they become more important to the plot than currently expected.

"There is one other," said Grandma Power at last, "who is crucial to our plans. He could not be here today, but he has been listening in with interest."

A voice boomed out of nowhere. Perhaps it echoed

up through the water upon which the meeting platform sat. "It is... important... doing something. We cannot, even, do nothing in this situation. I have asked Grandma Power to look into this before, and now... we must work together. For everyone. We must fight inequality. Between people, between galaxies."

"Hear, hear," said Zeddy Graves. "It's been going on far too long. I've done so much to fight inequality already, of course, so very, very much, but there's always more that others could do."

"I agree..." said the voice of Alex Burden. "I work every day for equality... No one seems to. Care? No. I fully support the plan of Grandma Power. This is a chance to change things forever. Change that is needed. Doesn't everyone think so? I do."

"Thank you, Alex," said Grandma Power. "Alex will lead the way in forming the peoples of our galaxy into one mind, one group, identifying those who are not on board and ensuring they are encouraged to find other places to live. Places where they will not trouble us."

"Thank you," said Alex. "That is all I want. What we want... Everyone thinking... the right thoughts... the right way."

"This has been a productive day," said Grandma Power. "We have come a long way. Never before have so many of the galaxy's most powerful people come together in one place without trying to kill each other. The next step is to make it official. I will hold discussions with each of you individually this evening, and then tomorrow we shall come together again for a grand banquet, where each of us shall present a dish from our home planets, as a token of our current co-operation and future friendship."

That didn't actually sound too bad to Pelney. He had never got to finish his strapple, after all. His tummy was beginning to rumble.

The Banquet That Doomed the Galaxy

Their night in the greatest hotel on the planet Nold had not been a peaceful one. Rolnikov had been certain that there would be an attack in the night. There was not, despite all the enemies they surely had on this world, but that hadn't stopped him waiting for it, pacing back and forth across the room as if he could outwalk his doom. Grandma Power had never shown up.

Pelney looked at the clothes that had been laid out for him. Someone clearly thought that his current attire was not suitable for the occasion. They were mad if they thought he'd wear another man's clothes in a situation like this. He didn't care about how he looked, at least not today, he cared about whether he would survive the day.

His clothes held many secrets! Secrets that had saved his life many times. What looked like a boring old tunic to you was so much more to him than that. What looked like dusty ragged trousers to you was an emergency kit for him. This may sound unlikely, but maybe we'll learn more about this later and you'll change your mind.

He pushed the clothes off the bed and onto the tiled floor, and laid down on top of them. He never slept well on mattresses, too used to the rigours of the open road. Maybe there would be time for forty-two winks before Rolnikov decided to leave.

The warrior of Uttar Pradesh was in the midst of his morning meditations, utterly naked, from his head down to his fingertips, on which he currently balanced. This was a crucial part of his daily routine, preparing his weaponised body for the day ahead, the fights that would surely ensue, the nastiness they seemed to attract like magnets. He was fine-tuning his muscles, calibrating response times, checking the organs of input and output were all up to scratch. There was no better fighter in the universe, at least so far as Pelney knew, but that didn't happen by accident or luck. It was the result of decades of hard work and practice, as success so often is. Of course, in Rolnikov's line of work, not many people get the opportunity to develop their talents over very many years.

Pelney closed his eyes and thought of home, on the far side of the galaxy. Melrune was not a safe, comfortable planet, but it was his planet, and he did not relish the times when the orders of the Orbiting Princess took them away from it. He was not used to interstellar travel, and would rather have left it to the professionals. Galaxonauts were a tough breed. Not, however, known for their diplomacy. Negotiations like this required both the steel of a Rolnikov and the slyness of a Pelney. Let them both be underestimated and the day would be theirs.

The one thing missing from Melrune was the most important thing of all: someone waiting for him to return.

He pushed that thought out of his head. It fell out of his ear and crawled towards the door, but he threw out a foot and squashed it flat. Must be getting sleepy, he thought, considering the oddness of his thoughts.

It was not to be!

"Time to go, Pelney," shouted Rolnikov.

Pelney opened his bleary eyes and pointed them in his friend's direction. The warrior was somehow fully dressed already, as if he had leapt to his feet and straight into his clothes.

"Do we have to?"

"If we don't, it might be the end of the world," said Rolnikov. "Who knows what those reprobates would do without us there. We should throw the lot of them into a pit of bottomless yearning. But if we can't do that, we must at least keep the peace for this meeting."

It was unusual for Rolnikov to talk at such length, so Pelney knew he must be serious.

We shall skip over some events quickly now, since by the end of this chapter we must have reached our cliffhanger, and our heroes have yet to leave the hotel. We won't even waste time describing the hotel, though it was very nice. They had breakfast, took a constitutional in the leafy grounds, and took the pre-arranged carpet to their destination. It felt a bit showy to Pelney. He'd have been happy with a rug or even a decent-sized mat, though as he stretched out and watched the desert pass by he had to admit it was pleasant to travel in style for once.

The banquet was to take place deep in the sands, where no enemy might approach without being spotted. Even an invisible foe would be given away by the sand they displaced. Such precautions were necessary, since each of the participants in the grand convocation would gain so much from the deaths of any of the others. Territory could be gained, power could be increased, money could be made. All it would take was one little betrayal.

But who would dare that, to turn the whole galaxy against them and their planet? That was the rock upon which this whole enterprise relied. More like sand, thought Pelney, as he watched it whizz by.

The carpet, driverless, guided itself by means mysterious to the squire, and soon they were there: a colossal purple tent, proudly incongruous upon the desert. It stood next to an oasis, pipes linking the two like the cord between a mother and her baby. The carpet dropped to land at the tent's entrance, then urged their disembarkation by trying to curl itself up. They complied, brushed off the sand that had attached itself to them in flight, and entered the tent.

The mood inside was cheerful. Each member of the nascent alliance was there, a friend or two in tow. Jack of Hands amused himself whittling an apple and looking around, keeping a weather eye on his new friends. Stentor Ploxton was being furiously friendly with a chap in yellow trousers. Zeddy Graves was dancing to music only she could hear. Jonana Cassandrus was moving from one attendee to the next, introducing herself and then immediately making her excuses, explaining that she had more important things to do. Grandma Power had not yet arrived, but the party was in full swing.

Pelney wasn't sure that he had wanted them to get on *quite* so well. This could lead to problems sooner rather than later, he began to feel.

Aside from a drape at one end that presumably concealed the lavatorial facilities, and another at the opposite end that, from the smells within, hid the cooking of food, the tent was not partitioned, it was one large hot room. Canvas, the same purple as the rest of the tent, protected them from the sand beneath

"Rolnikov thought back to the City That Faced the Stars, and wept"
Illustration: John Greenwood

their feet. Around the perimeter of the room were a series of long trestle tables, laid with spoons, ladels and carving knives, but as yet free of food. For once that suited Pelney. He had only just eaten breakfast and when the food came he wanted to enjoy it. There was going to be one meal from each delegate, a taste of their homeworld to share, a symbol of their newfound friendship and, in the eating, a literal demonstration of trust.

"Looks like fun," the squire said.

"Everything I dreamt of as a boy," replied Rolnikov.

Pelney laughed. "I should go and check on the progress of our meal." The Orbiting Princess had arranged for the transportation of the food from Melrune, and for its final preparation here on Nold by expert local cuisiniers. "Try not to cause any trouble."

Rolnikov nodded and went to stand with Jack of Hands. They had nothing to talk about, and so they did not. That suited the two of them very well.

Happy to see his colleague making friends, Pelney headed for the kitchens. Inside all was chaos, three dozen cooks in a whirl of chopping, mixing, bruising and brawling, and twice as many smells doing the same, a battle for scent supremacy. This would have been enough to make him feel hungry even if he were in the middle of stuffing his face with the fourth turkey of the day.

He struggled to get the attention of anyone, but at last was successful. "Where is the food from Melrune?" he asked.

The chef blew out his cheeks and harrumphed. "What do they make there, dung beetle soup? Maggot rind consommé? Rat finger *amuse-bouches*? Don't waste my time."

He tried to hurry off. Pelney persisted, placing one foot firmly on the chef's.

"I appreciate that our food is not the most

celebrated in the galaxy, but it is honest, delicious, and helps to produce strong fellows like my chum Rolnikov, mad knight of Uttar Pradesh. Should I ask him in here to make your acquaintaince?"

"That won't be necessary," said the chef, straightening his hat. "The food from Melrune is over there, at the tent's edge."

Pelney smiled and released the chef's foot. "Thank you! I hope our future interactions can be equally productive."

From what Pelney could tell, the cooking went well. The carcass of an entire exomentarius was roasting, doused in barbecurious sauce with a sprinkling of paprikanisters over its back. At its side a vast cauldron of thinly sliced potato chips fried, sizzling happily to themselves. He made a note to thank the Orbiting Princess specially on his return. She had deliberately sent his favourite meal, the perfect reward for this tiresome trip. In fact, he said it out loud: "When you get back to Melrune, thank the Orbiting Princess." That way he would remember thinking it, he would remember saying it, and he would remember hearing it. Triple whammy!

Pelney returned to the main part of the tent. Though no food had as yet emerged from the kitchens, there was plenty to drink. Alcohol from every edge of the galaxy! The juices of a thousand fruits! And hot sweet cofftea, the favourite drink of every battle-weary soldier! Pelney asked the sprawn server for a glass of whatever he or she thought best, and sipped it while waiting to see what would happen.

"Hello there," said Jonana Cassandrus, approaching from the side so quickly that he didn't see her coming. "Isn't it splendid for us all to be here together?"

Pelney nodded. "It is, although obviously I have my reservations about the situation–"

She held up a hand to stop him. "I'm sorry, I have to

go, I was supposed to be talking to somebody else, but I will see you later. Do enjoy the banquet."

You approached me, thought Pelney, I was trying to be polite. Never mind, he told himself. Perhaps Rolnikov had the right idea, speaking hardly at all and watching for trouble. But it was important for them to get a sense of whether this peace agreement was likely to hold, and, if so, for how long. He decided to risk his ears in conversation with Stentor Ploxton, and approached the group which was listening to him hold forth.

"We have been organising alliances for years," Ploxton bellowed. "There were seventeen of us in the Powerful Plenary five years ago. We conquered half the galaxy. But do they ask us how to do it now? No. But they want our help."

"The Powerful Plenary was nine years ago not five," replied Pelney, whose good intentions were so often undone by his pleasure in winning conversational duels. "And you conquered only eight systems before Ibis put a stop to those shenanigans. You should keep your facts straight. A spirit level might help."

"Yes, master," said Ploxton with a snarl.

"In fact," said Pelney, warming to his subject, one he knew well from long evenings spent reading on the Orbiting Princess's satellite while the Princess and Rolnikov sat quietly looking into space and not talking about their feelings, "when Ibis began to take the Powerful Plenary apart, they were shocked by how easy it was. None of you shared information with each other, you hated your allies as much as anyone else, and your approach to any problem was to shout at it until it went away – or until it didn't, and that's where your problems began."

Ploxton was fuming; it was obvious from the colour of his cheeks. Unless that was down to the half-empty flagon of Bentine Beer in his hand. Who knows what would have come next, if a troupe of juggling catrobats hadn't entered the tent and begun their performance.

Pelney clapped and cheered as they tumbled and frolicked, and inconspicuously made his way over to Rolnikov. He was always reasonably confident of winning a conversation, less so of winning a fight. Ploxton might be an obnoxious bullying blowhard with a distant relationship with the truth, but he was also one of the galaxy's most dangerous men. It wouldn't do to be attacked by him while Rolnikov was distracted.

The dazzling performance was over all too soon, but then it was time for the meals to be brought out and laid on the trestle tables.

"Still no sign of Grandma Power," said Rolnikov.

"A grand entrance, perhaps? She's making us wait, letting us know who is in charge. Or maybe her carpet began to unravel and she's waiting for a new one."

"Possibly," said the warrior.

The food emerged with the ceremony one might expect for a king or a queen or at least a well-known viscount.

The Great Brutish Bake-Off

First out were several huge trays of geometric shapes covered in various numbers of black dots. Pelney had no idea what they might be. There were pyramids, cubes, dodecahedrons and many others. As the trays were laid upon a table (to a great cheer from all around), Stentor Ploxton stepped forward with a grandiloquent wave.

"For those who don't know, these are a great delicacy of my world Chemicalia, an example of our proficiency in all things scientific and probabilistic." He took one of them in his right hand and brandished it at everyone in the tent. "This is a burzel. Roll them like dice, and see what comes up!" He shook the burzel in his hand and rolled it on the table. It was a three. "A different flavour every time!" He popped it in his mouth and grinned, wolfishly. "Steak!"

Pelney didn't much like Ploxton, but he would eat his food. He followed the crowd to the table and picked up three of the burzels, all cubes. The first he rolled came up four, and tasted of peach. The second he rolled came up one, and tasted of beer. The third he rolled came up four, and also tasted of peach. He felt silly to be disappointed.

Rolnikov didn't try the food.

The next delicacy to be presented was that from Jonana Cassandrus. About twenty casserole dishes were brought in, each of them full of a suspiciously red soup, from which emerged a quietly groaning plant, its multifurcated stems waving around as if to escape, and on the end of every stem a small, grey brain.

"These brainplants are perfectly safe to eat," said Cassandrus. "And do not feel guilty, the brains were not the plants' to begin with. They were stolen from rodents and other small animals that strayed too close to these fabulously frightful flora and put to work for the plants' benefit. You can pluck the brains and eat them like a fruit, and in doing so you save them from a disembodied half-life of slavery. You will do them a favour, a very tasty favour, a flavourful favour, especially since we have let the brainplants drink in a lovely *red* sauce." She winked in a highly suggestive way, plucked a little brain from the plant and took a huge bite. "Delicious!" she said through her chews.

Pelney applauded politely but gave Rolnikov a nudge in the table's direction. No way was he going to eat blood-flavoured squirrel brains. The warrior rolled his eyes but went to get himself a brain. Eating the food was a part of the treaty. There was no option but for one of them to eat it. Pelney couldn't tell if Rolnikov enjoyed the brain, but at least he didn't cause a diplomatic incident.

"Before we move on," said the disembodied voice of Alex Burden, "has anyone news... information... of... regarding Grandma Power? She should be here for this banquet. Or am I the only one who cares?"

Everyone shook their heads and shrugged, trying to look as innocent as anyone possibly could with bits of brain in their teeth.

"She didn't think it important enough to come," yelled Stentor Ploxton. "So why should we?"

"Cool it dudes," said Zeddy Graves. "Let's just enjoy the food and look forward to the future. I could be writing twenty hit songs today, but instead I'm here chilling with you all. We've got business to think of. Let me bring out my food. I think you're all going to like it."

She clapped her hands together. Pelney assumed there was a gadget of some kind concealed in her palm, since it sounded like a thunderbolt. From the kitchen came the pitter-patter of tiny feet, and into the tent came a rush of little creatures, crimson fruits running on little legs.

"Leggyberries!" sang Zeddy, and the leggyberries joined her in song, though they had no visible mouths to sing from. "La la lo, la la li," she sang, and they echoed it in their own way: "Lo lo lo, li la li!"

One ran up to Pelney and tipped its "head" to him. He plucked the berry and took a bite. It was very fruity, and it continued to sing as he chewed, its notes becoming increasingly melancholic. The legs curled up on the canvas floor and began to disintegrate.

"What do you think?" asked Zeddy, while staring weirdly at the decoration on a serving tray. She seemed even further out of it than usual. Pelney looked at the tray too. Three stone figures against a yellow background. He felt very tired, all of a sudden, but shook his head and pulled himself together.

"Yummy," he said. "I think I'll have another."

The next meal to come was Alex Burden's, the bearded banana. Neither Pelney nor Rolnikov were at all keen to try the food of a galactic-level criminal who was not in the room to pay with his life for any trickery, and it's not as if the bearded banana – pretty much what the name would suggest, a banana with a grizzly grey beard – looked particularly appetising.

"One of us better try it," said Rolnikov. "To show good faith."

"I have an idea," said Pelney. He approached the tureen in which the banana sat and sliced off a piece with his knife, before wrapping it up in a napkin and slipping it into a pocket. "This piece of bearded banana shall be eaten by the Orbiting Princess herself," he announced loudly, "to show her faith in this alliance. Now for the food from our world, Melrune, as selected by our mistress."

The other delegates looked rather relieved that no one would be asked to eat the bearded banana. From the kitchen now came the roast exomentarius, looking as tasty as anything in the universe ever had. A buzz ran around the room. Berries, brains and dice had their place, but this was a main course, worthy of a Grand Convocation!

"First dibs," said Pelney, rushing forward to slice off a healthy chunk. Diplomacy be damned, he wanted the best bit and he wanted to eat it now!

The others followed his lead, licking their lips with relish, all except Zeddy Graves, who turned away with a tut, apparently disgruntled that her leggyberries had been outshone.

If the roast exomentarius was popular, the fries produced ecstasy. Perfectly golden, crisp without being too tough, thin slices of hot sunshine, they were shovelled into mouths all around like coal on a steam train. Pelney and Rolnikov gave each other a nod. It looked as if their job had been done. Soon they would be away from this planet and on their way home, passing through the network of magical teleports that had brought them all the way here.

Unfortunately, that was not to be. The first sign that something was wrong came from the direction of Jonana Cassandrus, a horrified yelp. "By all the gods of Envia!" she squealed.

"What is it?" said Pelney, worried.

Her response was to point at him in accusation. "Guards, put your hands upon these two betrayers!"

Pelney looked at Rolnikov in confusion, and Rolnikov shrugged as if to say, what did you expect? There were not any guards around to follow her instructions, not really, just a handful of serving sprawns, but the criminal masterminds and their companions began to gather around the party from Melrune. Jack of Hands tossed the whittled apple over to land at Pelney's feet. It was now the shape of a skull.

"What is it, Jonana?" asked Stentor Ploxton in a tone that almost emulated concern. "What have they done?"

She pushed her fingers into the food on her plate, rooted around a bit, and pulled out the glasses of Grandma Power.

"They cooked Grandma Power and fed her to us. And they made her delicious!"

There was instant chaos.

"Traitors! Betrayal!" shouted Stentor Ploxton, slapping out a summons on a mobile messager.

Jack of Hands threw a knife in the direction of Rolnikov, who took a step to the side and caught it in mid-air, eliciting a nod of appreciation from the assassin, who then slipped out of the tent.

Others were running in, attracted by the brouhaha, weapons in hand. The canvas under their feet began to erupt in slices, masked warriors coming up from the ground.

"It's an ambush!" said Pelney.

"Someone expected this," answered Rolnikov, slicing off the arm of an attacker. He spun around Pelney, shoulder to shoulder, keeping his friend safe and the enemies at bay.

"Stop this!" called Pelney. "We had nothing to do with this! Why would we want to kill her?"

"You didn't want peace," said Zeddy Graves, "and you're not going to get it." She slapped her hand upon her hip and disappeared, instantly, with not even a flash.

"This isn't over," said Stentor Ploxton, by the look of it deciding too that this was no longer a safe situation. "You will pay for this, Rolnikov, and so will your world, and all of your friends." He popped a pill into his mouth, washed it down with the last of his latest beer, and was gone in a puff of indigo smoke.

That just left Jonana Cassandrus, the indignant voice of Alex Burden demanding to know what was happening, an increasingly large pile of bodies in a circle around Rolnikov and Pelney, and a handful of surviving leggyberries running around the tent trilling at the top of their range.

"I know you're enjoying yourself, Rolnikov, but we need to get out of here," said Pelney. "We need to get back to Melrune. They're going to need us."

Rolnikov nodded. "But how? We're in the middle of a desert, surrounded by enemies, and we got here on a chartered carpet. We got to this planet via a magical network of portals that is now blocked." Talking of which, he blocked a sword thrust aimed at his head and snapped the blade in two with a delicate counter-thrust of his own. From the tiredness in his attacker's eyes, Rolnikov deduced he was the father of a very young child, and he declined to make the killing blow, settling instead for kicking the guy in the knees. "I'm open to your suggestions."

Pelney closed his eyes, pressed his fingers to his temples, and had a quick think. "Okay," he said, raising his voice to be heard above the clatter of steel. "I've got an idea, but you're not going to like it."

"Will my doomed blade get to drink the blood of criminals and villains?" asked Rolnikov.

"Yes."

"Then I like it. Let's go."

Stephen Theaker's reviews, interviews and articles have appeared in Interzone, Black Static, Prism and the BFS Journal, as well as clogging up our pages. He shares his home with three slightly smaller Theakers, no longer runs the British Fantasy Awards, and works in legal and medical publishing.

On Loan

Howard Watts

Agent 1 was down, bleeding heavily from the gash in her side, colouring the library's oak floor. Her weapon far out of reach, her lance sliced in two – everything had happened so fast. If she hadn't jumped back in that instant the Principal had spliced into our stream, she'd have been cut in two. Advancing, the bulky creature was almost upon her, aware victory was close. Glowing with anticipation, its eyes narrowed, raising its sword, the blade as wide as my chest.

"*Return!*" I shouted to her as I ran forward, pulling the lance from my back, charging its field. She reached for her Marker, pulling it from the pouch on her belt, turning it over in her hands through blurred vision, fumbling for the controls. It slipped from her hands, the oval device rolling across the floor out of reach to come to rest against the far stone wall with a brief but final clatter.

My lance spat and crackled, calibrating itself, calculating our co-ordinates as its high-pitched whine grew. Just one touch of its field and the Principal would be instantly returned whence it came, *if* I could get close enough without being cut in half. Agent 1 held her wound with her left hand for a moment, then looked at her palm, breathing rapid and heavy. So much blood. Her eyes found mine, the desperation we shared – the overwhelming realisation of probable defeat and imminent death at the hands of this giant monstrosity, the Principal. As best she could she pulled herself along the floor, away from the beast, toward her weapon. But the effort was too much and she sank into unconsciousness. Her wrist-mounted Caregiver detected her loss of blood and her unconsciousness and she vanished instantly, returned to the House as the Principal's sword bit into the floor sending splinters of oak and splatters of blood into the air where she had lain dying a second before. The creature turned to me as it pulled the blade effortlessly from the wood, bellowing with anger, uttering some unintelligible other-dimensional obscenity as it pointed accusingly with a stubby talon, its features contorting, half resembling an expression of mocking hatred, I decided.

I stood my ground, fearful, trembling, my mouth as dry as the oak beneath my feet. I held out the lance, the first time I'd used it in actual combat, its charge building with an acrid odour of ancient electricity, masking the library's musty aroma. For some reason, right now, at this moment, my mind swam forward across the centuries to that fateful lunchtime conversation of a few weeks ago. It had been an innocuous chat at the bar that had delivered me into this life-threatening circumstance, with multiple realities – and my life – at stake.

I took a sip from my pint. "My dad warned me when I was a kid, telling me of how he'd loaned out a few of his seventy-eight LPs to a friend when he was roughly my age, and how they were returned to him, edges of the sleeves bent or creased, some heavily scratched. Worst case, a couple of these thick, brittle records had small nicks taken out of their edges, where his friend had picked them up like a dinner plate with thumb and forefinger. They were essentially unplayable."

Ray puffed a thick cloud of grey with his e-cig and

hastily waved it away. He watched the billowing smoke dissipate then turned to me, tapping the e-cig down onto the bar mat a couple of times for emphasis. "People have absolutely *no* respect for other people's property!"

"Yeah, I remember the regret in dad's eyes as he told me that story, and he concluded with a Shakespeare quote: *'Never a lender nor a borrower be,'* or something like that." I guess Shakespeare was talking about money – not records, but dad was fond of adapting quotes to suit the life lessons he eagerly imparted to me. As Ray drained his pint and ordered another I began to think about the lessons our parents teach us, how they struggle to emphasise their importance, and how for the most part we choose to ignore them, preferring to find out for ourselves, at our own cost. Our lunch time conversation reminded me it was this ignorant bravado that had cost me one of my favourite books around two years ago.

Ray took his change, fanning it out on the Devonshire Hotel's mahogany bar in order to assemble the correct coins for his third pint.

"Ray, have you ever loaned out a book and not got it back?"

"Many times," he said without looking up, pairing the coins and counting. "Do you want a half?"

"Thanks mate."

He picked up a few coins and passed them to Tasha before looking up to the ceiling, as if his next sentence was written there. "Loaned books, yes, mostly study books." His gaze returned to his pint. "When I was at university in Edinburgh." He held out his palms as the e-cig dangled from his mouth, wide-eyed with animated explanation. "It didn't matter, as I'd no *use* for the majority of them, and study books were expensive back then – so I helped out a couple of fellow students." He puffed again and thanked Tasha as she placed the half in front of me.

I nodded my thanks and spoke. "There was one book I lent out to someone, when I lived in London, before I moved down here. Never got it back. I had a mate that I used to talk to in my local and he loved SF, so I passed on this book to him. I saw him a couple of times after lending it and he promised to start it when he'd finished the two books he was reading at the time. Then I didn't see him for a couple of months and then I moved. I'd love to get that book back." I poured my half into my pint glass.

"Why don't you just buy another copy?"

"Not the point – I want *my* book back – even if it does come back like one of dad's records, although missing pages would be a no-no. As you said, it's my property. I can't even remember where I got it from. I *think* I picked it up in a charity shop."

Ray nodded and raised his eyebrows, fidgeting on his barstool, his eyes narrowing for a moment as his smoke found them. "Charity shops are great for picking up cheap books. Did you know I used to write short stories, had one printed in the university magazine? I keep reminding myself I should get back into writing, but it's difficult having to look after mum all the time." He tapped the bar with his e-cig again, snapping back to the present and facing me. "So, this book you leant out, what was it called?"

"*The Liar of Truths.*"

Ray shook his head after a few moments of consideration. "Never heard of it, who wrote it?"

"Oh I can't remember," I said quickly and with a little annoyance, then thumbed my phone and hit a Google search for the title. I passed the phone over to him.

"Mm. No results found," said Ray, under his breath.

He passed the phone back and picked up his pint and grinned. "Are you *sure* you've got the title right, Steve?"

"Positive. Although I've tried eBay, AbeBooks – no luck."

"Well, you could always try the library in town. They have a link to the British Library's entire catalogue. *If* you have the title right, they'll have a record of it."

I glanced at my watch. "I've got to go soon mate, I'll pop into the library tomorrow and let you know when I see you."

The town's library had been rebuilt a couple of years ago. It was a fairly sterile building, pastel shades, a few framed prints by local artists, chrome handrails, beech bookshelves, warm lighting – a typical council-funded building. I found a vacant PC and created an account. It turned out that the British Library's catalogue was accessible from its website. I searched for my missing book, and after a few seconds it offered a long list of books, but not the one I was looking for. I wondered if I'd remembered the title correctly. As I stared at the screen thinking about possible word combinations, a flash ad blinked down the right hand side of the page.

LOOKING FOR THAT ELUSIVE TITLE?

LOOK NO FURTHER. 1000000s OF BOOKS IN STOCK! – 100% SUCCESS RATE!

TRY *"THE MUSEUM OF MANUSCRIPTS"* NOW!

Daft name, I thought – but what did I have to lose? I clicked the link, expecting to find an elaborate site depicting rare books and most importantly a search window, but was greeted simply by a mobile phone number. I wrote it down, deciding to call after work.

"You've reached The Museum of Manuscripts. We're sorry, but all our representatives are busy right now. If

you would like to visit us personally to discuss your literary needs, please feel free to do so. We're open between eight and eight, seven days a week. Take the lift to the third floor, our address is..."

I wrote down the details and looked it up in Google street view. It was a central London address, so I decided I'd treat myself to a day out in my old home city the following Saturday.

It was a handsome little building, situated in a narrow alleyway called Raven Row, just off of a side street from the Charing Cross Road. The shop was double fronted, with panes of leaded glass windows roughly A4 in size either side of thin double doors, and I noticed how the glass of the bay windows curved gracefully at the edges allowing the passer-by a glimpse of the shop's offerings as they walked along the tapered pavement. The building looked as though it had been built in the 1800s, and I wondered at its original purpose. It could very well have sold sweets, cakes, bread or millinery. I took a step back into the road and looked up. Beside the doors which were reached by three steep stone steps stood proud Doric pillars supporting a balcony of broken wrought iron filigree where blacked-out sash windows reflected the faceless office building opposite. No signage sat above the shop front, and I wondered if the shop still existed as a viable entity. A bike courier rang her bell and I stepped back onto the pavement as she sped past, and as I peered through the dirty glass panes I noticed a few books strewn haphazardly across oak display shelves. A dim yellow light from inside hinted at possible occupation, and while London buzzed beyond this comparatively silent alleyway with traffic noise, taxi horns and the throb of thousands of Londoners around me, I knocked a couple of times then pushed the doors open.

A single naked light bulb decorated with cobwebs

hung from a cracked and damp stained ceiling rose to illuminate the silence. The shop was empty save for newspapers faded and curled upon the floor, a few pieces of broken furniture, empty bookcases lying on their backs. Peeling wallpaper created a camouflage pattern of neglect against the cracked plaster.

"Hello, anyone home?" I stood silently waiting for a reply, but the building ate my voice, refusing to respond with even the slightest echo, and as I took a few steps into the room I noticed an old caged lift, its concertinaed doors shut, its hollow carcass embraced by a flight of stairs with treads and risers intermittently vacant or broken. The building's original purpose immediately became apparent; it had been a hotel, no doubt an expensive and somewhat exclusive residence, serving actors, actresses and other theatre folk as they performed their various duties in the theatres along the adjacent Charing Cross Road.

Snapping back to reality, I swore under my breath. The lance was *still* collating information, and the Principal now sneered, bellowing a cry of triumph. I'd asked them at the House; *"Don't you think my training's been far too brief for such a mission?"* But they'd insisted. *"Agents are spread thinly across the realms,"* they'd said with conviction, *"with an experienced Agent at your side, the mission will be nothing more than an on-site training exercise."* Some cake walk. I cursed them again as the Principal sheathed his sword, turning his attention to the Marker my associate had dropped, side stepping with its huge gait to stand between me and the little object. For a creature of such ungainly bulk and size it then moved swiftly across the room, and within mere seconds the Marker was scooped up in its talons. I ran forward, the lance now charged but I was too late. The Principal nodded once – a thank

you I decided – just before vanishing. The Agent's
Marker had been set for the House, but I knew from
the brief conversations I'd had with other Agents that
Principals understood a little of our technology. I
cursed myself now. I should have thought to destroy
the Marker as soon as the Agent was called home. The
creature was now at the House, and I realised there
was no way to tell which Chapter it had decided upon
for its destination. It would wreak havoc. If I couldn't
return with a warning it could possibly eradicate the
entire staff in the departure hall. Forcing myself to
relax a little, I powered down the lance, realising I had
nothing left to do but retrieve the book, our mission in
the first place. Looking up to the tall arched windows
the night was slowly evaporating into morning as
birdsong filtered into the silence. The town would
soon wake, the library would open and if discovered
I'd have to explain my presence, and the blood upon
the floor. That would be impossible, as dialect training
wasn't given for this brief jaunt. I began quickly
searching the bookcases; looking for a simple atlas of
sorts, a tome illustrating some long forgotten
coastline. As the passing of time and the rising of sea
levels walked hand in hand together across the
centuries, towns and villages forming the south coast
had either been swallowed by the rising tides, or
pulled into the sea by coastal erosion, even in this
century. As Agent 1 had told me just before we'd
departed, somewhere, in one of these now long
forgotten sunken towns was a library. In that library
was a sealed vault, and in that vault a book, our next
objective.

I pulled the lift door aside, it coughed dust and debris
as it screeched in its tracks and I stepped inside. Floor
3. Great, there were buttons for floors 1 and 2, but

not 3. I wondered if I had in fact been misled – either by the telephone message, or by Google maps. Then it occurred to me. Don't ask me how, but I realised if I pushed the buttons for floors 1 and 2 together...

The lift shuddered, as if it had been woken from a long sleep. It dipped a couple of times then slowly ascended into the darkness. When it stopped I hesitated, wondering what on earth I'd find behind the door beyond the lift. Shrugging, I pushed the screeching lift door open.

The landing – if that's what it was – was well lit, and my eyes took a few seconds to adjust. I found myself on a black and white chequered floor of polished marble tiles. Either side the walls were lined with oak panels, highly polished too, with a hint of beeswax colouring the air. Ahead, what looked like an old railway station ticket kiosk – a brass plate with a brass bell alongside. I was relieved to see a sign above:

THE MUSEUM OF MANUSCRIPTS

Please ring for service.

The bell gave a bright but brief note as I hit it with my palm. I waited a few moments, hearing rapid footsteps click-clacking as they approached. They ceased and the shutter behind the grille slid upward. A woman stood there, tall, neat black hair combed back, white blouse perfectly pressed with a tight fitting scarf of red silk. Her face, quite heavily made up, seemed emotionless, lip gloss matching her scarf, her eyes hiding behind horn rimmed glasses, thick lenses with tortoiseshell frames giving her an air of superiority.

She spoke in a dusty grey monotone. "Do you have an ISBN number?"

"Er, no – sorry. I..."

She picked up a fountain pen from an inkwell, reaching under the counter with her other hand to produce a piece of paper, then wrote a line of numbers, speaking again. "Author?"

I recognised her voice from the answering machine message. "No, sorry – I just have a title."

She sighed and looked over the rim of her glasses, waggling the pen impatiently in the air above the paper between thumb and index finger. "Go on."

"The Liar of Truths."

The pen stopped and she set it down, removing her glasses slowly, placing them on the paper, clasping her hands together as she leant forward, her nose almost touching the grille between us. "Could you repeat that title, please?"

"The Liar of Truths," I said quickly. "I'm sorry but I don't know the author. It's a great..."

I realised every time she moved I felt as though she had interrupted me. She reached under the desk again to produce an old black Bakelite telephone, carefully placing it to her left, before lifting the receiver and dialling the number 1. The mechanisms whirred and clicked, then a brief pause.

"Front desk. Yes. Success, volume 1 identified."

I could just hear a voice on the line speaking excitedly; she looked up at me, studying me as though she was looking at a photograph. "Male, early to mid-thirties. Band C income bracket by the attire. Average, judging speech pattern, possible 2.1 above in all other categories." The voice spoke again on the other end of the line and she smiled, "Yes, Understood, thank you." She replaced the receiver and returned the telephone beneath the counter, producing another piece of paper which she slid under the grating along with her fountain pen. "If you'd be so kind as to write your full details for us, we'll be in touch. One of our representatives will see you at their earliest convenience."

Without giving it much thought I wrote down my

name, address, email and mobile number and passed the pen and paper back to her. She studied my writing briefly before folding the paper in half. "Thank you and good day," and with that she slammed down the shutter.

I wasn't having much luck for an "*on-site training exercise*", as the volume was nowhere to be found. With the loss of Agent 1 my search time was halved, my experience, zero. I discovered very quickly libraries in the 1500s were notable for their collections of cookery books. If the atlas had been residing in a private collection, such as *Johann Froben's* in Switzerland, or *Aldus Manutius'* in Venice, then the mission would have been simply one of buying, and perhaps a little sightseeing too. But no, the atlas had to reside here in the Corpus Christi College Library in Cambridge. As I searched among the shelves I realised what a contradictory time in history the 1500s are – libraries were becoming more and more popular, as the movers and shakers of the time realised information was valuable, and retaining it to share with others, essential. Yet for all this noble effort and social progression, this society feared the unknown, and anyone exhibiting behaviour beyond that of the accepted norm was accused of witchcraft. I allowed myself a grin. If I was discovered, accused and convicted of practising the dark arts (and heaven knows my clothing and equipment could not be construed as anything *but* dark) then at least I'd have a wide range of last meals to choose from in the pages of these cookery books. At last I found the atlas, and as I placed it carefully in my satchel I felt a weight rest upon my right shoulder, a glint from the polished metal catching my eye amid the dust. It was the blade of a rapier.

The train journey home was thankfully swift. I hurried to the seafront and into my little second floor flat, dropped my keys into the wooden bowl on the hallway table and walked into the front room.

"Good day."

I jumped and shouted in surprise at the sight of a grey-suited figure sitting in my armchair.

"*What the hell are you doing – how did you get in here?*"

The stranger stood slowly, offering his hand. "I understand you gave your details at the office – the Museum of Manuscripts – the file clerk at reception told you we'd be in touch. Stephen, isn't it?"

I found myself shaking his hand and nodding, my mind full of questions. "I'm the Proof-reader," he said confidently. He appeared to be in his early sixties, deep lines of age carved into his pale skin, long grey straggly hair, black shirt open at the neck. His eyes were alert though, bright blue and watery, but with a sadness to them.

He sat back down slowly. "Do you have any tea? I'm really quite parched – a cup and saucer would be lovely. White one sugar?"

"Yes, I mean – what the hell's going on here?"

"We're simply responding to your request to track down *The Liar of Truths*. We do have a reputation to maintain, Stephen. The Publisher and his staff work hard to ensure a blot free copybook. Please, forgive my intrusion, but this is an important matter to all of us and time's precious. How about that tea?"

I found myself in the kitchen filling the kettle as the Proof-reader joined me.

As I plugged the kettle in and flicked the switch I spoke. "You mentioned the Publisher – did they publish *The Liar of Truths*?"

"He, the Publisher, oversees all fictitious

publications, with my assistance. We ensure all works are suitable for the readership, and contain the correct measured messages, reading between the lines, as I do."

I made the tea, passing him a cup, saucer and spoon, wishing I'd stopped at the off-licence on the way home for a bottle of ale.

He smiled and nodded his thanks, his head tilting towards the doorway. "Shall we continue this conversation in the comfort of the lounge?"

We sat, he occupying my armchair and leaving me to the couch. He wiped the spoon with a handkerchief produced from his trouser pocket then stirred the tea slowly, tapping the spoon a couple of times on the rim of the cup and placing it gently on the saucer before continuing. "You see, Stephen, the Publisher and his Agents have been searching for *The Liar of Truths* for quite some time. We're well aware of the novel – it's a great read, and we don't blame you at all for sharing it." He brought the cup to his nose and sniffed once. "In fact we encourage lending."

"So why is it so important to you? Is it out of print, a rare signed first edition, low numbered print run or something?"

He smiled and sipped the tea, nodding briefly then licking his lips. "Out of print?" He allowed himself a grin. "No, not at all. In fact, it's not due for publication for another seventeen years."

I sighed, slapping the seat cushions either side of me with both hands. "This is *stupid*. How can you know about a book that's going to be published in seventeen years' time?"

He sat forward, placing the cup and saucer upon the coffee table between us. His tired face became stern. "I'll explain. You see ever since the very first published book of fiction, every book's influence upon its readership is measurable. Each and every story affects the reader in countless ways. Books are a subtle social controlling device, and it's up to the Publisher to ensure these messages and influences upon the public are for the good of everyone."

I sat back, aware the couch was far more comfortable than the train. "You're suggesting books have that much impact?"

"I'm not suggesting anything of the sort; I'm stating it as fact, Stephen. Authors hold great power at their fingertips – yet the majority without agendas or axes to grind are unaware of such. Throughout the centuries storytellers have caused the fabric of societies to alter in so many different ways, to take many twists and turns, to tear and fade and fold, ultimately leading mankind up to this very moment in time." He grinned again and clicked his fingers. "There, you see? That moment's gone, and in that moment hundreds of novels have been written, read and published, worldwide." He picked up the cup and saucer and sat back crossing his legs, cradling the tea in his lap. "The Publisher realised this, oh, several hundred years from now, at a time when the planet was on its knees through conflict and neglect. 'Where did it all go wrong?' many asked. Well, the heavy influences were traced back through history, and those influences were found to be contained in books." He tapped his temple twice. "New ideas, new ways to behave, to think, to work, to love, and to hate. Millions and millions of concepts and philosophies, circulating, being discussed, agreed, argued, fought over, debated and ultimately acted upon. Some works forced a change for the worst, so the Publisher decided to re-write every single work of influencing literature, to change the stimuli upon mankind, to establish the safety you enjoy now."

"But how can that be right? Surely you're interfering with the natural order of things – what gives you the *right* to shoehorn society into the way you think's correct?"

He blinked slowly and took a deep breath, I could see he didn't appreciate the criticism.

"With assistance from myself and a few like-minded individuals, the Publisher created the Editor, an engineered being able to digest huge amounts of literary data. The Editor is able to simulate how reality would be, if a few simple editorial changes were made to various works of fiction – works that had been responsible for creating our dark reality and the bridge built across realities by the Plagiarist." He drank deeply, draining the cup and placing it on the coffee table. "Perfect temperature, many thanks." I opened my mouth to speak but he cut me off. "Stephen, the publisher's reach is far – he has spliced his Agents into the past, altering every work that required a re-write to ultimately create the proud and noble reality you enjoy today." He nodded toward the coffee table. "And of course, that rather marvellous tea."

I shook my head. "So, you're telling me fiction has that much impact on society?"

"At the risk of repeating myself, yes. But let's be clear, my department is simply fiction." He waved a hand absently in dismissal. "There are other departments to deal with the other genres. Travel guides can be interesting, which I worked upon for a century or so, enticing tourists all over the globe in thousands of directions to thousands of destinations that were safe – but don't ask me about crime fiction – so many chicken and egg ideas there, so many novels responsible for planting ideas into the heads of psychopathic fools. Historical romance can be thought-provoking, but I'm hoping to spend my last century as head of screenplay editing. The weather's so much better out there on the East coast – although the tea isn't, I'm told."

"I don't understand, so how does this all fit in with *The Liar of Truths*?"

Well, that's the problem you see, my department's not entirely sure yet – the Editor is still collating information, running probable scenarios. Saying that, it's clear the book should not have appeared in advance of its publication date. Its influence has caused quite an upset already." He pointed at me briefly. "Your timeline has altered considerably following your reading it. If it wasn't for that book – a book that celebrates the benefits of living on the coast in several subliminal passages, you'd still be living and working in London. So your presence there is missed along with all your interactions." He sat forward, his eyes finding and intensity and determination. "We need to find that book, Stephen, discover whom you loaned it to, and see if that person still has it or has loaned it on again. Without this information the Editor is groping in the dark – having this book out there on loan revises everything."

I found it disturbing my life had taken a turn without my direction – a subconscious driver at my wheel of fate while I occupied a back seat staring vacantly out of the window as life sped past, all due to reading a book. "So what do you want me to do?"

He reached into his pocket and passed me a small oval object the size of my palm. As I took it, the mid-afternoon sunlight played across its glossy black surface. It was warm in my hands and as I turned it over I found an indent running around its circumference. At what I assumed to be the top of the object's circumference was a recessed gold button. I pressed it and the object slowly slid open, revealing a small keypad and three smaller gold buttons.

"Your Marker, Stephen," said the Proof-reader leaning further forward. "It's a traveller's bookmark providing almost instantaneous travel to destinations throughout history's pages, along with the comfort of our House, which is reached by the centre button. The Publisher thinks it best you meet him in person, as there's more for you to know – and an offer of employment in our esteemed organisation, if you're interested?"

I looked up. "Employment?"

He smiled broadly. "There's not many employers that can state, '*see the world*' in their job descriptions to the extent *we* can offer." He pointed. "If you're honestly interested, press the middle button on your Marker, now – no obligation following your meeting – but I'm confident" – he glanced out of the window – "you'll not look back to today, Stephen." He stood and nodded to the Marker in my hand.

After everything I'd been told I realised as I stared down to my palm I'd been given a lifeline with this small black device. I'd read the forbidden text, so to speak, and every waking hour with every interaction I undertook I influenced others. I was now part of the Publisher's problem. But, I'd been offered a career rather than a job. I just wished I could have had the time to tell Ray over a couple of lunchtime pints. I took a deep breath, changing my life forever as I depressed the button.

I watched without moving as the blade slowly retreated from my shoulder, my body tensing, expecting a thrust in my back, or a dagger drawn swiftly across my throat.

"Do you have the atlas?" came a whisper.

"I do."

"Then it's time to return."

I span around as I recognised the voice to see Agent 1 smiling up at me. "We must leave immediately," she said, sheathing her sword and glancing swiftly behind her. "Once the atlas is examined I'm certain the next volume will be far more difficult for us to retrieve."

"Home – the Principal – I couldn't…"

She shook her head, smiling thinly as her eyes closed momentarily. She gripped my forearms tightly and shook them once. "It wasn't your fault. Medical patched me up. It took a week of recuperation and I have a nasty scar, that's all. The Principal was slain – he'd spliced twenty years into our future, when today's exploits were old news. They were ready for him – or more accurately we were, as soon as he appeared," she grinned, "The look on his face!"

I sighed with relief and keyed my Marker.

"*I don't know!* It was a guy I met in a pub – he loved SF, he…"

The Publisher held up both palms and spoke slowly in a practised, measured rhythm. "SF, the Plagiarist's playground. Without SF, well, the Editor hasn't worked that reality out, yet." I stood upon a dias situated in the centre of the Publisher's study, a circular amphitheatre. He sat behind a huge curved desk, seemingly carved from a single piece of alabaster, reached by a flight of a dozen or so stone steps that encircled me. Either side of him, behind him and in front of the desk were piles of papers of differing sizes. Some were faded, dry to the point of crumbling into confetti, others held in ring binders, vinyl sleeves and card pockets. Behind him a valley of bookcases vanished to a point as far as my eyes could see, and here and there along these valley walls figures stood upon ladders of varying heights, replacing and removing books. Identical valleys – perhaps twenty or so – fanned out from the amphitheatre like spokes from a wheel.

"That's the second time I've heard mention of the Plagiarist, who is that?" I said.

The Publisher held my gaze as a figure approached him from one of the bookcase valleys to place a book in front of him. He nodded his thanks, opened up the book carefully to read, speaking at the same time. "Dreams are but electrical energy, energy that on occasion finds its way through natural fissures into other dimensions, similar realities to ours. Certain authors remember such experiences upon waking, and some include these visits in their fiction. Likewise, the Plagiarist inhabiting one of these dimensions feeds off these shared experiences. He interacts with the energy of our dreams as it briefly shares and nourishes his dimension." He turned a page, smoothing it down to continue. "The Plagiarist has grown from this, creating other realities to dominate. Look at all the alternate history novels." He glanced up. "No doubt you've read a few?"

"A couple, I guess."

"They, for the most part are *not* fiction, they are based upon actual alternate realities authors have visited and experienced during sleep, remembered and written down. I'm sure you've heard every noble writer has a pen and paper on their bedside table? You see, the Plagiarist is aware of my work, it interferes with his realities, contradicts them, alters them as we edit the works needed, so he instructs his Principals, his Agents, to remove certain books from our publishing record." His gaze fell to the book before him once more. "These works are *essential*, as not only are they core influences; they stimulate readers into becoming authors. Without those new authors and their work, well, I'm sure you can work the rest out for yourself, bearing in mind the information you've been given?"

My silence was all he needed.

"Then you'll join us?"

It sounded like a demand. "Why, why me?"

"You can track yourself down, once you're spliced in roughly the correct two or so years. You'll be able to observe yourself, remember your activities. Once you identify the person you passed *The Liar of Truths* to, other Agents can intercept the tome and return it to the slush pile before it's read. It's then just a matter of tracking down how the book found itself seventeen years ahead of its assigned publication date. We'll leave that to our most senior Agents. Well?"

"Do I have a choice?"

He returned to the book upon his desk. "The Proof-reader is waiting for you at reception. You'll be given a briefing and one week's training.

The Dias descended.

Training wasn't that difficult. There was no need for dialect integration, just a few reminders of custom and practice – but they were hardly needed as I was only going back there to observe and report – and it was just a couple of years ago.

The time passed slowly, and I soon became bored watching myself. I found myself wondering at my mission and the point of it all. As the Publisher had pointed out, a more senior team would take care of *The Liar of Truths* appearance, so why didn't they just do that in the first place, saving me the boredom of following myself around? It was obviously a ploy to study my dedication to my new occupation as a junior Agent, as this mission wasn't that essential in the scheme of things.

Finally the day came when I watched myself pass the book over to a friend in the pub. I followed him home, took down the co-ordinates with my lance and spliced home.

The mission was a complete success, the book removed before it could be read by my friend, but I realised I still carried the influence of its narration, its plots, conflicts and characters around in my head like an infection. I wondered if I would be imprisoned in solitary confinement by the Publisher and his organisation until the book was released. But no, his solution was far kinder. I was called to his study following my second mission to retrieve an atlas from the 1500s.

"The loop is almost closed," he said with great satisfaction. "The origin of *The Liar of Truths*' premature appearance has been identified, the situation nullified. Agent 1's debrief following your search for the atlas confirms the appearance of a Principal, spliced in at almost the exact moment you both arrived at the Corpus Christi College Library in Cambridge, June 21st, 1528. It was that same Principal that appropriated a copy of *The Liar of Truths*, before the creature came here in an attempt to wreak havoc. The Marker retrieved from his body confirms his arrival was his *third* splice with the device. The first – a trip some eighteen years hence, where he'd simply seized any book he could, to supplant it into the past. A very simple but extremely effective ploy, resulting in you finding *The Liar of Truths,* in, as your statement says, 'a charity shop'. "

I remembered my first encounter with that Principal, the way it had pointed and spoken to me in the library all those hundreds of years ago, its mocking expression, its unintelligible vocalisations – they were now clear to me – they were signs of recognition. The creature had waited and waited, ensuring the book had been purchased. It had seen me purchase the book in the charity shop, then spliced to Home, the final part of his plan.

"There's just one small factor to eliminate, and then we're on schedule."

I knew what he was talking about.

"Your interactions must be limited until the book is

in circulation. You cannot involve yourself with any member of the population, lest you infect them with your knowledge. For this reason, your status as Agent is effective immediately, and you'll be placed on permanent active duty from this moment forward. To eliminate any possible contamination, you will submit to having the memory of your life following the reading of the impurity erased, should you inadvertently interact. You will not remember any knowledge of *The Liar of Truths*, your lifestyle inherited from that read, your change of address and the resulting interactions will not take place. You will spend the rest of your life working for me and my cause."

It was a one man job, an easy couple of day's work for a change. The weather was guaranteed great, so I dressed accordingly and hit the button on my Marker. I booked a room in a small hotel – the Publisher telling me there was a very small chance of a Principal's incursion. I'd never seen one in broad daylight – not since the late 1900s, in almost twenty years splicing. Still, you could never predict them, so I carried standard equipment for the trip.

It was a small launch by any standard – a limited guest list, the usual crowd; the free drinks and canapés groupies. I queued along with everyone else, the Proof-reader telling me to blend in – as if I needed telling – and what better way than to join a queue? Besides, the Publisher had told me I should get myself a copy for my collection of first editions – not that the author was going to follow it up with anything else worthwhile in his relatively short-lived career – no movie or TV deals for this writer – just this one hit, which kind of put this place on the map and turned him into a cult figure, so I'm told.

I picked up a copy from the pile, handing over a thirty which covered the book and the signing and waited my turn.

The author seemed genuinely pleased to see everyone, he shook their hands, giving a wide smile as he shakily inscribed every copy.

"Hello, who shall I make it out to?"

"Steve, please."

He signed and I took the book, shaking his offered hand briefly as the queue shuffled impatiently behind me.

I sat in the bar situated next to the function room for a while, keeping my eyes on the two entrances as I made small talk with the bar staff and sipped a pint of ale. No sign of a Principal. The function soon came to a close, guests shook hands and waved their goodbyes, fans chatted, drank too much then made their excuses filtering out into the early summer evening. After a short while the author entered the bar with his small entourage. He looked pleased, but exhausted as he sat on a stool down the bar from me. I opened the book he'd signed. *To Steve, best wishes, Ray.* I glanced up, watching the author as he ordered a pint and puffed a cloud of smoke with nervous satisfaction from his e-cig. *The Liar of Truths.* Strange title, I thought, frowning. I closed the book, eager to splice home. Perhaps I'll read it one day, when I get the time.

Howard Watts is a writer, artist and composer living in Seaford who also provides the wraparound cover art for this issue. His artwork can be seen in its native resolution on his deviantart page: hswatts.deviantart.com. His novel The Master of Clouds is available on Kindle.

The Battle Word

Les Aventures fantastiques de Beatrice et Veronique

Antonella Coriander

Captain Vorta and Commander Borra were given no choice in the matter. Easy-going and friendly as the Haddisses generally were, the word of the Great Egg was law. They were led to the spaceport, where a large domed cage was being erected by three dozen Haddisses working in concert.

"This is where you will have to fight each other," said Flight Commander Zigglesward. "I like you both very much and had looked forward to working with you for years to come, invasion permitting. I'm really most awfully sorry."

Borra really thought she was, though it didn't help. By the end of the day the cage was complete and Haddisses of all sizes and shapes surrounded it with burning torches in hand. Vorta and Borra were pushed inside.

They were in fact pushed inside together, through the very same opening. An awkward moment came, as each wondered whether to take the first step away from the other: for that would be the first acknowledgement that they would indeed fight.

There was no cheering, no baying for blood, no baring of teeth. This was a solemn duty, a requirement, an unfortunate consequence of their world's desperation.

"They can't make us fight," said Commander Borra.

"They have their ways," answered the captain. "See the sharpened poles surrounding the dome? If we do not fight, they will slowly move inwards. No one will push them: it's just a matter of time, an unwinding coil of vine. We will both die. And the Haddisses will be left without a leader."

"That's down to them," said Borra, unconsciously taking a step away, then becoming conscious of it. It did sound like Vorta was ready to fight her if necessary. "They could let us out at any time."

"And face the wrath of the Great Egg? Well, I say wrath. It would just be grumpy with us for a bit. But it does give us this advice for a reason. It's always turned out to be right before. Especially when we've ignored it."

That was enough for Borra. She ran to the other side of the cage and turned to face the captain warily. "You're not going to fight me, are you?"

"What do you think?"

Borra wasn't sure. How long had she known the captain? She didn't yet remember her previous existence on Haddis or the original journey to Earth. But they had spent a short period together in space, travelling back from Earth. Before that an even briefer time in the cybernet, as Veronique and Brzk909. And she remembered their adventures together as Beatrice and Veronique on the island of the crystal wizard. In all that time she had taken their comradeship for granted. It had felt right. Natural. Surely the explanation for that comradeship could be found in their pre-existing, half-forgotten (her half, that is) relationship as captain and commander?

"I trust you, Captain Vorta."

"Then we must fight."

In other circumstances, the captain would have won the fight without breaking a sweat. Borra was still not fully used to this body, and was certainly not able to make full use of the cage's vertical aspects. Her tail just would not do what she told it to, and she was afraid to fully extend her claws in case she hurt herself.

But the captain had one disadvantage. The youngling. Buried down deep in her underpouch for protection. Still too young to be taken from her mother, even in a deadly fight to the death.

It made the fighting difficult. Neither one wished to land a killing blow, but the danger was that even a relatively soft contact could have hurt the youngling.

"Have you given her a name yet?" asked Borra, after one exchange of scratches.

"No," said Captain Vorta, lashing out with her tail and catching Borra on the upper right knee. "I cannot – urg! – believe she is real. Have you seen her cuteness? I have done nothing to deserve that."

Borra waited for the captain to try again with her tail, and this time stepped quickly forward to catch it behind the knee, clamping down her tail to hold it. She might not be able to move her tail with the accuracy and delicacy of the captain, but it was strong and squeezing hard did not take much control. The captain groaned with pain as Borra twisted to force her to the concrete ground.

"You do yourself a disservice, Captain Vorta. And your daughter. Perhaps a name that reflects where she was born?"

"In space, you mean?" said the captain, struggling to get free. "Good idea. The human word for the stars is 'star'. I shall call her Starla."

"Lovely," said Borra, before coming in tight to press her advantage. Around the cage came sad sighs of anticipation. "Now," she whispered to the captain, "what is your plan? Breaking out of here and running for the ship?"

Captain Vorta shook her head. "We would be caught before we got anywhere."

"Then faking a death. The other would be led away, and the apparent corpse could then get up and leave."

"Impossible," said Captain Vorta. "The ruse would be rumbled as soon as the body was checked."

"What then? If we must fight for real to escape this, I will let you win. You have a daughter." It occurred then to Borra that perhaps she did too. But could she really have forgotten something as important as that, whatever she had been put through?

"To be honest," said Vorta, "I was really hoping an opportunity would present itself by now. I thought maybe the flight commander would call it off or something."

Borra became worried that little Starla might get squashed beneath them, so she rolled away, miming the pain of receiving a blow to her face. The captain got slowly to her feet, and the two stared at each other from a distance, slowly swaying with fatigue.

"We cannot fight for real," said the captain. "In this I know the Great Egg to be wrong. The strength of Haddis is in our friendship, our love for one another, our loyalty. Anyone can make a mistake, even the Great Egg."

Borra took a moment to look around the spaceport. It was almost impossible to discern anything in the darkness beyond the ring of torches that surrounded them, but against one horizon a familiar silhouette was blotting out some stars.

Their spaceship!

Was it close enough?

If it wasn't, it would hardly make things worse. A bit of social embarrassment was nothing compared to taking a pointy stick in the guts!

She yelled, as loudly as this new body of hers would allow – which was pretty darn loudly: "Computer, I need you!"

A polite voice rang out across the spaceport, causing consternation among those watching the fight. "Commander Borra? How can I help?"

It had heard!

She waited for a lull in the anxious shouts that were the first reply to the computer's words, then shouted again herself. "Rip the lid off this cage, will you? An extraordinarily cute little youngling is in danger here, not to mention her mother! And me!"

"Of course!" replied the computer. "Be right there!"

In a few Haddissy seconds the spaceship had lifted off. It breezed across the top of the cage, scraping off enough to open up a hole without bringing the whole thing down on their heads. Then it drifted back and dangled its ladder down into the cage.

"All aboard!" the computer called.

Captain and commander moved quickly, scampering up the ladder with all the haste that was due – from the corners of their eyes they could see their former colleagues climbing the outer sides of the dome. There was no anger in them, just concern that the Great Egg's instructions were not going to be followed.

Inside the spaceship, the ladder was retracted and the hatch closed. Knocks and bangs could be heard as the Haddisses tried to get their attention, but the three space travellers were safe, at least until someone thought to bring weaponry more potent than torches to bear upon the ship.

"Where to, Captain?" asked the computer.

Captain Vorta shrugged. She reached down into her underpouch and lifted out Starla, cradling her and washing away the youngling's tears with her tongue.

Borra took a moment to enjoy the sight of mother and daughter, out of danger, precious and together.

Then it was time for action!

Borra stood to her full height and addressed the computer. "We go to the Great Egg!"

Compared to the trip from which they had just returned, the journey across town to the Great Egg was nothing. She was looking at the Egg almost before she had finished taking the breath that followed her order. On the viewscreen the computer had put up for her, the Great Egg looked much smaller.

"That trick with the cage," said Captain Vorta, popping the gurgling youngling back into her underpouch. "Do it again with the Great Egg."

"Are you sure?" asked the computer, awe in its voice.

"It must be done," said Borra.

And so the Great Egg was cracked.

Borra and Vorta dropped through the hatch and down the ladder, landing on the topmost platform inside the Great Egg, coming face to whatever with the yolk itself.

"What have you done?" boomed the Great Egg.

"What had to be done," replied the captain. "You have led us wisely, Great Egg, but we cannot abandon our very natures in pursuit of victory."

The Great Egg's voice deepened. "Even though it doom your species?"

"Even then," said Borra. "And we have been to Earth. We saw no evidence on the cybernet of invasion plans."

"Think back," replied the Great Egg. "Think back, to your time in slowsuits, as Beatrice and Veronique, on the island of the crystal wizard."

"You mean the wizard?" shouted Borra. "She plans to invade this planet? We defeated her!"

"No," said the Great Egg. "You drove her away from

one base. That is not the same thing. Regardless. Is this your final decision, then? Do you refuse to fight?"

"I do," said Captain Vorta.

"I do," said Commander Barra.

"I do," said Starla from deep within Vorta's underpouch. Haddisses learn to speak quite rapidly. (Like humans, it takes them rather longer to learn how to think.) The two friends looked at each other and shared a moment of exquisite happiness, all the more special for presumably being their last.

"Then I have no option," boomed the Great Egg, as Haddisses piled onto the platform, weapons pointed their way, "but to accept that you have passed my test."

Vorta and Barra, expecting obliteration, were not surprised to find their consciousnesses falling into darkness, but they were puzzled by the Great Egg's last words.

"You shall protect my magical fairy castle!"

"Wake up, my darlings!" sang a sweet voice. "Time to wake up, no time to sleep, if you sleep you miss your treats!"

Beatrice struggled to do as she was told. She could feel that she was lying on a soft bed, and was not inclined to leave it. She was so exhausted that ever getting up again seemed like a distant prospect. Even opening her eyes proved difficult. But she managed to flutter her wings a bit.

That woke her up!

Wings!

Nothing could have kept her eyes closed at that point, not even a thousand elephants sitting upon her eyelids. And what she saw when they opened:

Standing at the side of her bed was a beautiful fairy queen, with long red hair in a braid that reached down to her ankles. She wore a long green dress that shimmered in the sun as if it could actually feel the sunlight bouncing off it. Around her neck there was a ruby amulet, and on her forehead was an emerald green bindi. She was smiling, and had eyes of kindest brown.

The bed was a four-poster, with green velvet drapes, silk sheets and a pile of quilted blankets. The rest of the room looked rather chilly, its stone floors and walls bare, save for a tapestry here and there.

A medieval castle?

The sky outside the window was blue, the brightest blue Beatrice had ever seen.

"Am I back on Earth?" asked Beatrice, lifting up her hands to look at them. No longer the robotic appendages of the crystal island, nor the trapezoids of the cybernet, nor the claws of Commander Borra. They were human hands again, and she had two of them.

"Silly Bea, of course you are on Earth!" The fairy queen laughed. Not a cruel or mocking laugh. One filled with joy and happiness. "This is the magical realm of Lovelyland!"

"Okay," said Beatrice, taking a deep breath. "This is going to take some getting used to."

Her next thought was to look for her friend, and there, to the left, just a couple of metres away, was a second four-poster bed. In it she could see Veronique, looking very much as she had done in what Beatrice remembered as their first encounter, in the skies above the English Channel. She looked human, and she had her legs – which had not agreed with the dinosaur that ate them! – back in place. There was one difference, though: curled up on Veronique's back were a pair of glistening fairy wings.

Beatrice opened her eyes wide, then sat up and reached around to her own back.

There they were! She had a pair of fairy wings of her own!

She ran her hands around her back and shoulders, searching for the harness that was keeping the wings on. Nothing! Her hand followed one wing's lower edge to its source. The wing seemed to sprout from her shoulder blades!

She looked carefully at the fairy queen. "Can I fly with these?"

"Of course you can, Beatrice, you silly!"

Beatrice had flown out of the window before the fairy queen even had time to suggest putting on warmer clothes. It was a chilly winter morning. Not exactly the time to go flying in a nightdress! But it hardly bothered Beatrice, who thought happily back to her bicycle rides as she swooped and soared, dived and turned. A couple of times she felt herself stalling, and worried that she might fall. However, her body knew what it was doing; each time, she moved unconsciously into a dive and gracefully bottomed out.

Despite the exuberance of her flying, she knew her reserves of energy were low, and so she did not fly far from the castle. From out here she could see just how lovely the fairy queen's castle was. Delicate purple spires rose at each corner, and a high wall protected it, as did a moat around the outside. The castle stood halfway up a mountain whose sides were thickly wooded. A single trail led up to the castle from the valley below.

"Who would ever want to attack such a lovely fairy queen?" wondered Beatrice, before she heard a scream come from the castle.

Veronique!

It took Beatrice a few attempts to find the right window: it was the crying that led her back. Veronique was sitting up in bed, sobbing her eyes out. Beatrice landed gently on the stone floor and ran delicately over to her friend.

"Veronique, what's wrong?" she asked.

Her friend looked at her with mingled shock and horror. "Where's my daughter, Beatrice? Starla? Where is she?"

The fairy queen was trying to comfort Veronique, yet if anything she was making it worse. "Veronique, my dear, you don't have a daughter. That was all part of the game."

"No!" shouted Veronique. "My daughter was not a game!" She got to her feet, acknowledging her wings with nothing save a scowl of irritation, and ran from the room.

"Veronique, wait!" called Beatrice, with no effect. She went to run after her friend, but the fairy queen laid a hand on her shoulder.

"It's quite natural, Beatrice. Don't worry." She took Beatrice's hand and led her slowly from the room. "She went too deeply into the illusion, and came to believe it. She thinks she really has a daughter – did she say Starla? – but of course she doesn't. She's been sleeping in bed for days, as have you, playing through my little test!"

Naturally, Beatrice had many questions about all of that. Her first priority, however, was her friend. She shook off the fairy queen's hand and ran to find Veronique.

Only the echoes made it difficult, because Veronique was yelling at the top of her voice, as she entered every room and corridor and staircase, "Starla! Starla! Where are you, sweetheart?!"

It took just a minute for Veronique to reach her. She didn't try to stop her friend, or hold her back. She didn't speak. She just helped her search, because she understood why it had to be done. Wherever they went, through store rooms and banquet halls, kitchens, bedrooms and libraries, fairy maids stood silently, watching them with sad eyes. Sometimes she saw the fairy queen, regarding them from a balcony or the top of a staircase. There was no sign of Starla, no sign of any children. Barring accidents, fairies live a long, long time. Their childhood is comparatively brief. Hence it is unusual to ever see fairy children.

Beatrice wondered what they were looking for, exactly: a fairy child, or a four-kneed, long-eared Haddis youngling?

At last, it seemed, Veronique had exhausted herself, and collapsed into Beatrice's arms. "I can't find her, Beatrice, I can't find her anywhere."

Beatrice led her to a couch, and sat her down. For a few minutes they sat without words, Veronique sobbing into Beatrice's shoulder.

At last Veronique sat up straight, and wiped her eyes with her nightdress. It wouldn't be accurate to say that she stopped crying. She paused it. Put it somewhere else so that she could do what had to be done.

"She was real, Beatrice, I know she was."

Beatrice held her hand. "She was beautiful."

Veronique almost laughed. "Even with those teeth!"

"Even with those teeth. And the four knees. And the long ears. And the tail. She had such lovely eyes."

Veronique shook her head. "I know she was real. Does this seem real to you? This fairy world?"

Beatrice looked around, and shrugged. "I don't know, Veronique. We've been through a lot. This feels real. But so did Haddis. So did the cybernet. So did the crystal island. So did flying on my bicycle. Maybe all of that was real, maybe none of it was. But that's just our surroundings. You and me, we're real. Our feelings are real. Whether Starla really existed or not, our love for her was real. Our friendship for each other is real."

Veronique nodded, keeping tears from her eyes by sheer force of will. "I will find her again, I know I will."

And Beatrice really believed she would.

The fairy queen chose that moment to enter the room. Perhaps she had been waiting discreetly outside. She pulled a second couch over to face them.

"I'm sorry that my little test hurt you, Veronique," she said. "My illusions have never before been so powerful. If they were always so strong, I would not have needed you to take the test in the first place. The casting of my spell must have coincided with a spike in solar magic rays. I doubt I could put you so far under again."

"What test?" asked Beatrice, not taking her eyes off her friend, whose hand she was still holding.

"I needed to know if the two of you were ready to defend our castle against the horde of the Toothpick Queen. She is sending them against us, and I feared we would not survive. Her illusions are so much more powerful than my own. We have one chance, a mighty weapon, but I needed to know that the fairies who would carry it could not be swayed from their purpose – and their friendship – by any illusion."

"So you created the world of Haddis?" asked Veronique.

"That's right – but not without your consent, my dear. I even played a role in it myself, as the Great Egg. I feel awful, now I realise how deep it went. I had to put you in a position where you were forced to fight each other, where it was the only way to survive. But you refused, you found another way. You are ready to defend us against the hordes of the Toothpick Queen! Whatever illusions she tries on you, I know you will stand strong!"

Veronique was silent for a moment. Then: "Did you create Starla?"

The fairy queen shook her head. "No, I did not. Sometimes... illusions gather a life of their own. Like a snowball rolling down a mountain. I choose the starting point, and can guide the illusion to some extent. But it all happens in your minds, and should you wish to take control, you always can. I draw the map, you choose the route. So no, Starla was not my idea. I wish I *could* take the credit – she was adorable."

That was just too much for Veronique. She began to cry again, though she turned away to hide it. She chewed down on her fist to stop herself bawling out loud.

The fairy queen closed her eyes, slowly, and then opened them again. "I'm sorry. Beatrice, Veronique. I'm so sorry. But you have important work to do this evening. I will have fairy maids bring you fairy food and fairy drink. Make yourselves ready, for at dusk the Toothpick hordes attack! Our lives are in your hands!"

"Do you know, I haven't even asked her name," said Beatrice.

Veronique looked at her. "The Fairy Queen, you mean?"

"Yes."

"I haven't either. Maybe that is her name. But look down. This isn't the best time for this conversation."

They were hundreds of metres up in the air, not far off being able to leap up and touch the clouds. Beatrice chose not to look down, not just yet. Hovering was tricky. She didn't want to break the spell.

"You're right, sorry," said Beatrice. "Let's save the castle, then worry about ourselves."

"And Starla," said Veronique, not making eye contact.

"And Starla," agreed Beatrice.

Veronique flew a loop around Beatrice. "Look at how well we use these wings. I don't remember being a fairy, but if I wasn't surely I'd find this difficult?"

Beatrice chose this moment to look down, and there

they were, in the distance, at the other end of the valley: the approaching hordes of the Toothpick Queen. From here they looked like ants swarming down a rumple in a big green tablecloth. But the fairy princess had warned Beatrice and Veronique what to expect up close. Siege towers, giants, dragons, ogres, soldiers, centaurs, demons, all made from toothpicks, and hence much sharper than your average army.

"And at the back," the Fairy Queen had said to them, "carried by a troop of her deadly bobby-pin battlers, the Toothpick Queen herself!"

If the Toothpick Queen was there, Beatrice couldn't make her out yet. But that was why they had been told to keep a careful watch from a distance. Within reach of the Toothpick Queen they would be subject to her magical attacks, as well as the ranged and melee attacks of her army.

"Let's get back down to the Fairy Queen and tell her they're on their way," said Veronique.

"At dusk, just as she predicted," replied Beatrice, following her friend down to the fairy castle.

The Fairy Queen was waiting for them on the battlements, resplendent in orange sari and wide straw hat. "Is she on her way?"

Beatrice and Veronique nodded.

"Come with me," said the Fairy Queen, and she led them along the battlements to where a pair of pretty young fairies in black and blue robes were wrestling something bulky and awkward out of a wooden crate.

The two fairy girls stopped their work and turned at their approach. One was a little shorter than the other, and wore her dark brown hair with a fringe. Her face was determined. If you could have dropped that face among the Toothpick Horde they would have run away, knowing that they could never overcome such determination!

The taller of the two had light brown hair, and had

obviously just begun to grow out her fringe, which was held up above her glasses by a kitten hair slide. This taller fairy girl seemed rather distracted, as if she was thinking very carefully about something else, something very important.

The Fairy Queen held out her hand to introduce the two fairy girls. "These are my two smartest fairies, Oreleil (in the glasses) and Elzeyt." Everyone said hello. "They have been working on our special surprise for the Toothpick Horde."

"Yes, that's right," said Elzeyt. "Thank you for volunteering for this mission, Beatrice and Veronique. I know it's dangerous."

"Yes," said Oreleil quickly. "So dangerous! It could all blow up in your face! You're very brave."

Beatrice and Veronique looked at each other and raised their eyebrows.

"Apparently we're the kind of brave people who volunteer for this kind of thing," said Beatrice.

"But it would have been nice," said Veronique, "if you could have put in that bit of extra effort to make it safe."

Oreleil burst into angry tears. "All the work I've done and that's what you say! That is so unfair! I haven't slept a fairy wink in fifteen days!"

Elzeyt walked over, gave Veronique a kick in the shins, and returned to her original position as if nothing had happened.

The two fairy girls held hands and stared at Beatrice and Veronique with the fury of a thousand rattlesnakes. For a moment. And then it was over.

Elzeyt broke the silence. "Carry this magical device to the Toothpick Horde and bathe them in its mystical rays. We call it the Magnificent Sunshiner."

"Do not let them get you down to ground level," said Oreleil. "The device will be ineffective down there."

"And the Toothpicks will rip you to bits," said Elzeyt.

She paused a second, as if daring Veronique to make a critical comment. Everyone held their breath. Elzeyt and Veronique stared at each other, the former intently, the latter with an ironic arch to her eyebrow.

Beatrice worried about Veronique. She had been wrenched away from her youngling – and then told the youngling had never even existed! Beatrice did not know how Veronique was managing to cope, but an ironic detachment seemed to help. Perhaps a similar disappointment had led to her life of crime in the first place.

Stop that! she told herself. There had been no life of crime, no chase over the English Channel. The Fairy Queen had told her so. It had all been a test, an illusion.

So why did she still feel, even in these fairy wings, like a police officer?

"How does that sound?" asked the Fairy Queen.

"Totally fine," replied Veronique. "Let's have a look at it."

The "device" inside the crate was a glowing sphere about a half-metre wide, cradled in a net of intertwined branches which extended to handles on either side – or at least they would once the thing was out of the crate. Veronique reached in to grab the handle on one side, and Beatrice reached in to take the handle on the other.

"One, two, three..." counted the two friends, and then it was out, and they were holding it between them. What was left to do, other than fly out to meet their enemies?

"This won't kill them?" asked Beatrice.

"Oh no!" said Oreleil and Elzeyt and the Fairy Queen together. It was Oreleil who continued: "Absolutely not, Beatrice. It will discombobulate, deconstruct and demolish them, but not destroy or kill. The toothpicks will return to what they were before the Toothpick Queen cast her spells on them. Toothpicks!"

"When you're done," said Elzeyt, "all the fairies of the castle will come out and gather up the toothpicks in bundles. The Fairy Queen will rent a boat and send them all home. No one will die! The very thought!"

Beatrice and Veronique counted again to three, and took off, heading immediately in the direction of the approaching Toothpick Horde.

"Remember," said Beatrice, "that the Toothpick Queen will attack us with illusions if we get within her range. And we will be within her range. Whatever we think we see, we mustn't dive down. We must stay up where the Magnificent Sunshiner can do its work!"

Veronique scowled at her. "I know all this."

"I know, it's just..." She didn't continue. She had thought Veronique might be distracted, and she didn't want to say why.

"Be a good friend and shut up, okay, Beatrice!"

"Got you, Veronique. Let's do this."

They flew from the castle down into the valley, soon realising that the horde's advance guard were further advanced than they had realised – some had almost reached the bottom of the trail that led to the castle!

Never mind. It provided them with test subjects.

Test subjects who collapsed to the ground in a tumble of toothpicks!

"It works!" yelled Veronique, provoking loud cheers from the direction of the castle.

Veronique and Beatrice, more confident now, headed for the main horde, swinging swiftly over any other advance parties and reducing them to toothpicks. A few minutes of flight and the Toothpick Horde was beneath them, a raging mass of angry wood. Catapults and arrows were fired in their direction, but they were far too high up for them to be reached by missiles.

The reverse was not true: the effects of their weapon reached the Toothpick Horde, no problem! Each pass over the army's heads wiped out a swathe of attackers, and despite the angry threats, howls and caterwauls that came from below, there were soon more toothpicks on the ground than on the march.

"Are you feeling the effects of the Toothpick Queen's magic yet?" asked Beatrice.

Veronique shook her head. "Nothing. Perhaps she isn't here."

But she was. There was her infamous toothpick carriage, drawn by toothpick unicorns, coming out of the woods and heading up the valley.

Beatrice and Veronique kept clear of her at first. No point taking the risk until the bulk of the army was finished. So they passed over the Toothpick Horde's heads again and again until they were all in pieces on the ground. That left just the Toothpick Queen. Fearing the worst, they flew over her carriage, and watched it fall apart just like the rest of her army.

There she was, sitting on the grass, wearing a dress of multi-coloured toothpicks, crying at the sight of her fallen army.

"Feeling anything yet?" It was Veronique's turn to ask.

"Nope. Do you think we should go down to talk to her?"

"It could be an illusion," said Veronique. "The Fairy Queen did warn us. Look at what she put us through in preparation. We should return to the castle."

But she knew they would not. This unhappy queen needed their help. Without another word spoken, they began to descend. They rested the Magnificent Sunshiner on the ground and approached the Toothpick Queen.

She saw them through her tears. She dug out a clod of earth and threw it in their direction. "Are you happy? Are you here to gloat? You've beaten us. Again. You fairies. How could you?"

Beatrice sat down in front of her. "I'm sorry. We're just trying to protect our castle from your attack. I don't think it's killed any of your friends."

"Oh, well, that's all right, then! Do you want a medal? You didn't kill these children. You just pushed them to the ground and knocked them unconscious! Well done! Very well done!"

"Children?" asked Veronique quietly.

"You especially, Veronique, how could you do this? Yes, children! What do you think they are?"

Beatrice looked around at the aftermath of their one-sided battle. "These are just toothpicks. You're the Toothpick Queen, aren't you?"

The woman's eyes went as wide as her face. "Is that what she's been telling you? You're under a glamour! A spell! Don't you know what you've done?"

She came over to them and laid her palm on their foreheads, first Beatrice and then Veronique.

Beatrice looked once again at the battlefield. The entire valley was covered with the sleeping bodies of scruffy, unarmed little children. She looked up to the fairy castle. It glowed with scarlet malevolence, and in the distance she heard an awful, mocking laughter.

Antonella Coriander is not so sure about this. *"The Battle Word" is the eighth episode of her ongoing Oulippean serial, Les aventures fantastiques de Beatrice et Veronique.*

MORPHEUS TALES

THE BEST WEIRD FICTION VOL 6

THE BEST WEIRD FICTION VOL 6

MORPHEUS TALES

"With Echoing Feet He Threaded"

The Two Husbands

Walt Brunston

"Husband Two, Husband Two!" shouts the crowd of journalists gathered outside the Husband Headquarters. There are at least forty-five of them, he counts at a glance, hustling and bustling to get their microphones and cameras as close to him as possible. It's all pointless in this day and age – thanks to the relentless march of electronic progress they could sit in a skyscraper three miles away and film him just as well – but viewers and readers like drama, and there's little as dramatic (or at least little as *predictably* dramatic) as getting face to face with a person returning to their home after a professional and personal disaster.

"Do you have a statement?" shouts one man, a green bowler hat upon his head. A strange detail to notice, thinks Husband Two, but then everything feels strange to him at the moment. Husband One is gone, perhaps forever.

"Do you now become Husband One?" yells a woman with a pink flower tucked behind her ear. He shakes his head while trying to walk past.

"If Husband One is dead, are you still a husband at

all?" asks an extremely tall journalist who looms over the pack.

"We do not discuss our private lives," says Husband Two with a scowl. That is their rule.

A journalist wearing a long brown trenchcoat has decided they've got everything they're going to get out of Husband Two, and has begun her piece to camera. He lends her half an ear while negotiating the crowd to cross the Husband Plaza.

"Husband Two has returned to the Husband Headquarters," she says into her microphone. "Alone. Husband One was lost in the course of an anachronistic bank robbery by the super-villain Tortoisio, formerly known as Professor Quigg, a contemporary of Professor Challenger."

Husband Two finds himself intrigued by her words, and imperceptibly slows his pace to hear more. Tuning out the shouts of the other journalists is difficult but he is well-practised in the careful use of his hearing. How many machines has he repaired by sound alone? A mere click in the wrong place is often all it takes to guide his spanners!

"There is immense curiosity in Pseudo City and beyond as to the precise nature of the relationship between the Two Husbands. Are they the husbands of each other? Or the husbands of other people? Are they widowers, fighting crime to avenge dead spouses? Or are they a couple, fighting crime together? No one knows, and they refuse to talk about it. Whatever the case, there is now just one husband in the headquarters. He has sworn to recover Husband One, but where will he start?"

Where indeed? wonders Husband Two. For a moment he considers inviting her inside, simply to have someone to help him think things through, but he dismisses the idea as daft within a second. Her goal would be to investigate the Two Husbands, not the disappearance of Husband One.

No, this must be faced alone, he decides. He waves to the Headquarters in a particular way and the plaza begins to gently lift. Prepared for it, he continues to walk forward with confidence, but the journalists are staggered, and then, as the gradient increases, are rolled softly back to the roadside.

Husband One turns, gives them a mockingly friendly wave of farewell, and steps into the Husband Headquarters through a second-floor window.

"Drat, drat, drat!" says Njna Wal, the top reporter for PCNN – Pseudo City News Now – the highest-rated and most prestigious news channel in the country. Back home she has a display case full of awards, and a mailbag full of publishers begging for her to write her memoirs. She covered all the big stories of the last five years. The President's peace treaty with the Outer Hebrides. The discovery of intelligent plankton in the San Francisco bay. Unearthing corruption at the Spelling Bee International. She's done it all. But one scoop evades her, again and again: the Two Husbands! What is their story? She won't rest easy until she finds out.

And now Husband Two thinks he can roll her out of the way like... like... a rotten log.

"A rotten log," she says with a snarl to Zey Thea, her camera operator. "Is that what he thinks of me?"

Her colleague shakes her head. "He's just got a lot to think about at the moment," she suggests.

"He needs to think again, Zey! I'm getting in there whatever it takes."

Zey knows better than to argue. "Let's go back to the news van and get you set up."

Husband Two's first step is to change into his favourite outfit. A dark blue boiler suit with enough pockets for everything he'll need. Two interlocking gold wedding rings are embroidered upon the breast pocket. He takes the lift to floor twenty-six of the second tower.

This is Husband Two's laboratory. He clears a space upon a workbench (not an inconsiderable task, since it involves transferring several pieces of delicate equipment, some of them so delicate that they can only be seen through a microscope). He sets Tortoisio's gun down upon the work bench and tries to make sense of it. A carved potato, a length of copper wire, and a sealed pack of playing cards. A close examination reveals nothing whatsoever. There are no hidden parts, no microchips embedded within the potato, no circuitry in the playing cards, no nanotechnology scurrying upon the copper wire. What could such a collection of junk possibly do? Nothing. Nothing at all.

But he has seen it send Husband One spiralling out of existence.

He needs to test it.

The tenth floor of the Husband Headquarters contains a shooting range, where the Two Husbands are able to experiment with the weapons they have captured, or, rather less frequently, the weapons they have created – non-lethal, of course.

(The Two Husbands try not to kill. There is not enough life in the universe as it is.)

This is where Husband Two takes the mysterious weapon of Tortoisio. He steps out of the lift and onto the range. It runs the entire width of the Husband Headquarters, across both Tower One and Tower Two.

Husband Two picks up a noise-dampening headset and puts it on. The gun made no noise when used in the bank, but he knows from experience that the devices of super-villains are highly unpredictable! He moves to the shooting range's control console, where he can select from several scenarios. Does he want to test himself, running around in mock-up buildings and shooting bad guys while not shooting innocents? Not this time. He goes for the simplest option, a single figure at medium range, and the room rearranges itself to suit his choice.

He raises the gun to chest height and prepares to fire, then thinks better of it and returns to the console. "Better safe than sorry," he says to himself. He asks the room to give him a bit of protection, and up pops a transparent shield with holes for his hands to pass through into protective gloves.

"Much better," he says, though he feels like a bit of a coward.

On the other side of the shield is a small shelf, and he puts Tortoisio's gun there before going back behind the shield and putting his hands through the holes into the gloves. It's more awkward to hold the gun this way, but if it blows up he'll stand at least a small chance of surviving. No point taking unnecessary risks. He wouldn't be able to save Husband One from inside a coffin.

He spends a few moments wondering whether that is actually true, and thinking about the technological means by which his brain could be kept alive and in touch with the world outside despite the death of his body, but soon realises that while it might theoretically be possible to try saving Husband One from inside a coffin, it would not be ideal.

He prepares to fire the gun, taking a deep breath and pulling gently on its trigger.

"Wait!" comes the shout. "Don't shoot!"

A woman steps out from behind the target figure. She is dressed in black from head to toe, and has brown skin and black hair. Husband Two recognises her.

"Njna Wal!" he shouts. "What are you doing here? Why shouldn't I shoot? I'm here to test the gun, and testing it on a human would be ideal."

She puts her hands in the air and begins to trot towards him. She comes to a quick stop when she realises that Husband Two is moving the gun to keep her in its sights.

"Would you stop that!" she calls. "Put it down."

He does not. "Answer my questions first. I assume you were taking notes and I do not need to repeat them."

"You're serious?" she says, putting her hands on her hips.

"I am never not."

She sighs and shakes her head. "In answer to your questions, then, in order. I am here to get the scoop on what has happened to Husband One, and to a lesser degree the scoop on the secrets of the Two Husbands."

"Prying as ever," says Husband Two.

She does not dignify that with a response. If heroes have the lives of all humanity in their hands on a monthly basis, it's only right that humanity should get to ask a few questions.

She continues. "You shouldn't shoot me because it would be murder. And you are not a murderer."

Husband Two shrugs. "I am not yet sure that Tortoisio's gun kills people. It may do nothing but transmogrify you, and as far as I am aware that is not yet a crime."

"And to answer your last question, yes, I was taking notes, and I think some of them may help you to find Husband One."

Husband Two puts the gun back down on the shelf and takes his hands out of the gloves. He steps out from behind the shield and walks over to the journalist.

"Okay, Njna, you have my attention! The Two Husbands aren't done yet!"

Walt Brunston's *adaptation of the classic television story,* Space University Trent: Hyperparasite, *is now available on Kindle.*

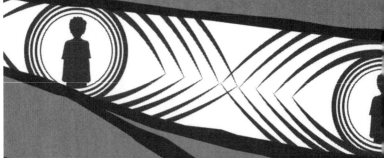

The Quarterly Review

Reviews by
Stephen Theaker,
Douglas J. Ogurek,
Jacob Edwards
and Rafe McGregor

Douglas J. Ogurek's *work has appeared in the BFS Journal, The Literary Review, Morpheus Tales, Gone Lawn, and several anthologies. He lives in a Chicago suburb with the woman whose husband he is and their pit bull Phlegmpus Bilesnot. Douglas's website can be found at: www.douglasjogurek.weebly.com.*

Jacob Edwards *also writes 42-word reviews for Derelict Space Sheep. This writer, poet and recovering lexiphanicist's website is at www.jacobedwards.id.au. He has a Facebook page at www.facebook. com/JacobEdwardsWriter, where he posts poems and the occasional oddity, and he can now be found on Twitter too: https://twitter.com/ToastyVogon.*

Rafe McGregor is the author of *The Value of Literature*, *The Architect of Murder*, five collections of short fiction, and over one hundred magazine articles, journal papers, and review essays. He lectures at the University of York and can be found online at https://twitter.com/rafemcgregor.

Stephen Theaker's reviews, articles and interviews have appeared in Interzone, Black Static, Prism and the BFS Journal, as well as clogging up our pages. He shares his home with three slightly smaller Theakers and works in legal and medical publishing.

We don't have a policy on ratings, other than that reviewers use them or not as they prefer!

Audio

Jago and Litefoot, Series 5, by Jonathan Morris, Marc Platt, Colin Brake and Justin Richards (Big Finish)

Professor Litefoot (played by Trevor Baxter) and theatre impressario Henry Gordon Jago (Christopher Benjamin) first appeared in "The Talons of Weng-Chiang", a popular *Doctor Who* story starring Tom Baker as the fourth Doctor, and made such an impression that a spin-off was reportedly considered. Good ideas never die, they just wait for their moment, and eventually Big Finish began this series of audio stories for these Victorian "investigators of infernal incidents". Best of all, their stories are now available on Audible, along with many other Big Finish titles. (I've already spent monthly tokens on *UNIT: Dominion* and the fourth Doctor Lost Stories box set.) Season five

puts a new spin on the format, thanks to the Doctor's
useless navigational skills. After taking the pair from
1893 to the New World and to Venus in a pair of very
entertaining specials, the sixth Doctor dropped them
off at home, but in the wrong century: they are now in
1968. These stories deliberately (as the special features
explain) skip over their initial acclimatisation to the
swinging sixties, to show them settled in their new
lives, and ready for new adventures. Litefoot is
working in an antiquarian bookshop, bought for him
by Ellie Higson (Lisa Bowerman), a friend from the old
days who has made the most of her vampiric longevity.
Jago is on the verge of becoming a television
personality, presenting an old-time talent show. Each
of the four episodes lasts about an hour. All are by
male writers, but Lisa Bowerman directs. Jonathan
Morris writes "The Age of Revolution", about a TV star,
"Timothy Vee off the TV!", and his peculiarly hypnotic
statue. "The Case of the Gluttonous Guru" by Marc
Platt is about the swami Sanjaya Starr, leader of the

temple of Transcendental Meditation, who is looking for a host for Mama, the Great Birth Mother... "The Bloodchild Codex" by Colin Brake sees Ellie get skittish as another vampire shows up on the scene, looking for a book in Litefoot's collection. "The Final Act" by Justin Richards confronts the pair with old enemies. Connections to the past are present throughout the stories thanks to the grand-daughter of the Great Godiva, Guinevere Godiva, who takes an uncommon interest in the crystal they brought back from Venus, and Detective Sergeant Dave Sacker, dogged descendant of another old friend. The four stories are all equally enjoyable, providing terrific dialogue for the two leads to wrap their wonderful voices around, with a sound mix that works just as well whether one is listening on earphones, a pillow speaker or a surround sound system – though obviously the latter was best. The audiobook also includes seventy minutes of special features. *Stephen Theaker* ★★★★☆

Books

The Book of Kane, by Karl Edward Wagner (SF Gateway)

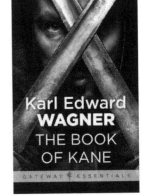

Kane is a warrior, big as two of his friends put together, three hundred pounds of bone and corded muscle, tremendously strong, startlingly agile, able to see in the dark, red-haired and left-handed. He is very long-lived, supposedly the son of the original Adam, and has in the course of that life accumulated many useful abilities, some of them mystical. Time to him has no meaning, "a dozen years or as many minutes – once past, both fitted into the same span of memory", and when he makes his entrance in a story, it is often a surprise to those who thought him long-dead, or just a legend. The five stories in this collection all find him in a pseudo-medieval setting, the longest, "Reflections for the Winter of My Soul", stranding him in an isolated castle threatened by highly organised wolves. Reading that story, one could think Kane a hero, but later stories make it clear than he is a thoroughly bad person, a rapist ("Raven's Eye") and a mass murderer of men, women and children ("The Other One"). In "Misericorde" we see him at at work as an assassin, while in "Sing a Last Song of Valdese" he plays a minor role in revenge being taken upon another gang of rapists and murderers. He isn't a character you can admire, and of course you don't have to always admire characters to enjoy reading about them, but "Raven's Eyrie" in particular makes for uncomfortably problematic reading, being apparently more dismayed by how Kane's victim let the trauma affect her than by the crime itself. Perhaps this story appears out of chronological order because as the first story it would have left readers much less sympathetic to its protagonist. The ebook does have rather odd pagination, with the first story beginning on page 187, the second beginning on page 83, the third on page 143, but is mostly free of the scanning errors that have plagued other SF Gateway titles. A book of fairly decent stories with a loathsome protagonist. *Stephen Theaker* ★★★☆☆

Murder on the Einstein Express and Other Stories, by Harun Šiljak (Springer Science and Fiction)

This title is part of a range intended to bring science and fiction together, which has familiar sf names Gregory Benford and Rudy Rucker on the editorial board. Their ethos is highly appealing: 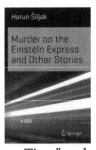 "Authored by practicing scientists as well as writers of hard science fiction, these books explore and exploit the borderlands beteen accepted science and its fictional counterpart." Unfortunately this book, a short collection of four stories – "Normed Trek", "Cantor Trilogy", "In Search of Future Time" and "Murder on the Einstein Express" – doesn't seem to have been copy edited or proofread. Articles definite and otherwise are frequently absent and tenses are often wobbly, making it a trial to read. If it hadn't have been short enough to read in a couple of hours I would have given up on it. The author is clearly very clever and an expert in his field, but he is trying to get across ideas that would at times be very difficult for the general reader to follow in even the clearest prose, and that isn't what we get. Not infrequently I was enlightened more by Kindle's lookup feature providing the appropriate Wikipedia page (e.g. for the Monty Hall problem) than by the explanations in the book itself. As for the stories themselves: I understood very little of "Normed Trek", but mathematicians may enjoy puzzling out its functions. "Cantor Trilogy" imagines a future where computers take over the writing and peer-reviewing of academic articles. I stumbled through "In Search of Future Time" without really understanding much more than that it seemed to concern the Turing Test. And "Murder on the Einstein Express" uses an extremely thin fictional frame to support a socratic canter through various thought experiments and puzzles. The author seems to acknowledge the book's flaws in this story, joking that "criticism of the author's literary style is strictly forbidden", and having a character say: "I have always enjoyed writing. The fact that I am not good at it couldn't stop me, since I had the will and thought it's enough." I feel much the same way about writing my own novels, but I would hope, if a professional publisher were to pick them up, that their editors would help me to remedy their shortcomings. *Stephen Theaker* ★☆☆☆☆

Note that the following Lone Wolf reviews were written and supplied before we heard the sad news of Joe Dever's death. Our commiserations to his family, and to all of his fans.

Lone Wolf 22: The Buccaneers of Shadaki, by Joe Dever (Mantikore Verlag/Holmgard Press)

In #55, I reviewed the collector's edition of *Lone Wolf 21: Voyage of the Moonstone*, published in English by Mantikore Verlag in 2015. The review was more of a reflection on the whole series, summarising the thirty years between my first reading of *Lone Wolf 1: Flight From the Dark* to the point where, after numerous improbable narrative twists, there once again seemed to be a delay in publishing. The short version: Lone Wolf was originally conceived as a series of thirty-two gamebooks, the first of which was published in 1984, stalled – apparently forever – in 1998 at *Lone Wolf 28: The Hunger of Sejanoz*, and has been the subject of many and varied attempts to both finish the series and return all its instalments to print. I concluded by noting that although Mantikore Verlag's taking over of the series from Mongoose Publishing in 2013 was an initial success, it seemed to have run into trouble in the second year. On 1 April 2016, shortly after I submitted the review, Joe Dever announced that he was self-publishing the rest of the collector's edition series, including the previously unpublished four books. I must admit I was disappointed by the news, after the heroic efforts the fans at Project Aon (www.projectaon.org), a non-profit organisation, had

made on Dever's behalf, but I'm pleased to report that
Holmgard Press (www.mapmagnamund.com) is
flourishing. *Lone Wolf 29: The Storms of Chai* (also
reviewed in this issue) was published in June and
Dever is also selling the Mantikore Verlag volumes that
are still in stock, books 18 and 22. Having suffered at
the hands of small presses on several occasions myself,
I'll add that I had no problems whatsoever with my
purchase of *The Storms of Chai* and that the price
(£17.95) includes postage and packaging in the UK. In
addition, all copies purchased from Holmgard Press
arrive with Dever's seal and signature (for those who
set store by such things).

Returning to *The Buccaneers of Shadaki*, my Kai
Grandmaster – True Friend – had put in the kind of
performance his wimpy name would lead one to
expect in his mission to return the Moonstone to the
Isle of Lorn and found himself in the city of Elzian at
the end of *Voyage of the Moonstone*. In my previous
review I mentioned that the gamebooks have moved
through distinct series as the overarching story
progressed: a single campaign in the Kai and
Magnakai series (books 1 through 12), followed by a
series of standalone adventures in the Grand Master
series (13 to 20) all with the same character, Lone Wolf.
Voyage of the Moonstone marked the beginning of the
fourth series, the New Order, in which the reader
adopts the persona of one of Lone Wolf's acolytes, and
it was not clear whether the twelve books of the New
Order would take the form of a single campaign or
more standalone adventures. Dever seems to be
employing a third, hybrid, option, with some New
Order missions being standalone and others spanning
more than one book (about which I shall have more to
say below). The second half of the Moonstone quest
takes True Friend "deep into the wild and lawless
reaches of southern Magnamund", which will only be

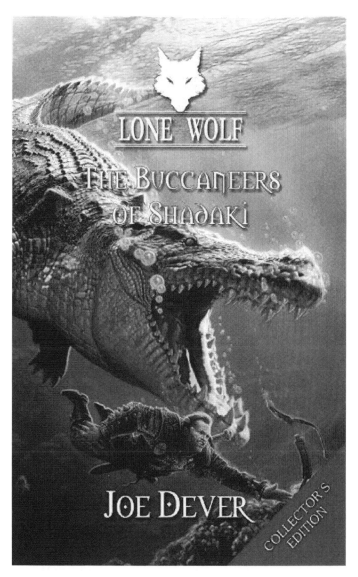

familiar to those readers who played Ian Page's regrettably short-lived spin-off series, The World of Lone Wolf (four gamebooks were published by Beaver Books from 1985 to 1986, beginning with *Grey Star the Wizard*).

This survey of the southern continent is the book's greatest strength and the narrative is a sequence of fascinating explorations of and mini-adventures in the ports between Elzian and Lorn: from the emporium of Zharloum to the junkyard that is Dlash-da Ralzuha to a run-in with Sesketera, the despot of Ghol-Tabras; from the ruined splendour of Caeno, with its famous guanza derby, to the austerity of Nhang, with its eighty stone statues, and finally the Port of Suhn, ruled by the wizard Grey Star (hero of *The World of Lone Wolf*). The southern continent of Magnamund is every bit as interesting as its northern counterpart, where Lone Wolf cut his teeth, but *The Buccaneers of Shadaki* is more of a guidebook than a gamebook, even if it is a guidebook no one should be without. The combat finale is with a Zhürc, which might be a sea dragon and might not – one cannot be certain because there is no illustration – and provides an anti-climax either way. The creature on the eye-catching cover, drawn by Manuel Leza Moreno, is a scary sea crocodile called a Nigumu-sa that appears much earlier on, between Ghol-Tabras and Masama, but despite its presence the adventure as a game is altogether too easy.

One of the problems that has emerged in the New Order series was evident in some of the Grandmaster series: when one is playing a single character, who advances in prowess and power with each adventure but who is not involved in a campaign – working his way through increasingly difficult minions of an evil archenemy, for example – it becomes difficult for the author to maintain both the peril factor and a minimal degree of realism. True Friend is a Kai Grandmaster Senior at the beginning of Lone Wolf 21, which means that he is advanced to twenty-five out of a maximum of thirty-six levels of expertise and has several supernatural abilities. If Dever had opted to make *The Buccaneers of Shadaki* more challenging, he would have had to put some pretty tough opponents in relatively innocuous settings – but it would be stretching the imagination too far if street thugs and hungry animals were capable of taking on one of the most fearsome warriors on the continent. This is one of the reasons that I prefer a campaign to a series of standalone adventures. Speaking of which, like all the other Mantikore Verlag/Holmgard Press collector's editions, this 574pp volume includes a bonus adventure, "A Wytch's Nightmare" (written by Vincent Lazzari and Alexander Kühnert). The reader's persona is the Wytch Yenna, her mission is to find the missing Grey Star, and the writers' use of a female protagonist makes a very welcome change (true to its eighties origins, the various Lone Wolf protagonists have hitherto been exclusively male).

As my next review will be of Lone Wolf 29, I shall conclude this one with a brief summary of books 23 to 28. *The Buccaneers of Shadaki* ends with the promise of "a new and sinister threat to the fragile peace of Magnamund". That threat is Baron Sadanzo and his robber-knights and *Mydnight's Hero* (#23, first published in 1995) sees True Friend assisting the exiled Prince of Siyen to reclaim his father's kingdom. *Rune War* (#24, 1995) returns the action to the Stornlands, a war-torn region in northern Magnamund where Lord Vandyan of Eldenora has used the Runes of Agarash to raise a reptilian breed of warrior. While Lone Wolf leads the crusade against Eldenora's army, True Friend must break into the fortress of Skull-Tor to destroy the runes and his success sees him rise to become the second most powerful Kai Grandmaster. Shortly after the victory against Eldenora, Lone Wolf is abducted by a necromancer named Xaol and True Friend rescues him from Gazad Helkona in *Trail of the Wolf* (#25, 1997). (Unfortunately, the plot of rescuing friends or allies has been a little over-employed in the series, especially if one includes the standalone graphic novel spin-off, *The Skull of Agarash*, published in 1994, and "A Wytch's Nightmare".) Meanwhile, the greedy Dwarves of Bor have dug too deep in search of wealth, released an ancient horror called the Shom'zaa, and require True Friend's assistance to defend their Throne Chamber in *The Fall of Blood Mountain* (#26, 1997). (As another aside, I should mention that this is currently the rarest of all the books; a second-hand copy was sold for just over £1000 on Amazon in August.) *Vampirium* (#27, 1998) takes a slight change of direction in that it initiates a series of events that will (it seems) dominate the remaining five books. The Autarch Sejanoz of Bhanar despatches a mission to excavate the Claw of Naar from the ruin of Naaros and True Friend must intercept the party before it returns to the capital. Sejanoz proceeds with the invasion of Chai without the Claw in *The Hunger of Sejanoz* (#28, 1998) and True Friend is sent to escort the Khea-Khan to safety. *The Hunger of Sejanoz* was published with only three hundred (as opposed to the usual three hundred and fifty) gameplay sections – I am not sure why – but Dever has plans to remedy this... all of which will be discussed in my review of *The Storms of Chai*. *Rafe McGregor*

Lone Wolf 29: The Storms of Chai, by Joe Dever (Holmgard Press)

In my review of *Lone Wolf 22: The Buccaneers of Shadaki* above I mentioned that Joe Dever is now self-publishing the Lone Wolf series of gamebooks, after close on twenty years of problems with first Red Fox, then Mongoose Publishing, and most recently German publisher Mantikore Verlag. One would have hoped that after all the trials and tribulations suffered by both Dever and his fans at the non-profit Project Aon

(www.projectaon.org), his decision to take charge of the process himself would have run smoothly, but alas this was not the case. *The Storms of Chai* is book 29 in the Lone Wolf series as a whole and the ninth adventure in the New Order series, which rebooted with a new player persona in *Lone Wolf 21: Voyage of the Moonstone* (reviewed in #55). The New Order series was published at the rate of two books a year from 1994 to 1998, by which reckoning *The Storms of Chai* would have been published in 1999. With Dever at the helm after seventeen years, the long-awaited adventure – which had been sold out on pre-orders – was due for release in April 2016. There was a delay with the printers and it seemed as if the Lone Wolf project had stalled yet again. The book was finally released in mid-May and with a stack of further pre-orders to meet, Dever ordered a second edition printed. In yet another improbable twist in the Lone Wolf story, a second first edition was printed and although the books are exactly the same, the difference in paper used by the Turkish (fat) and Lithuanian (thin) printers has resulted in the former being substantially thicker and heavier than the latter (Dever explains the full story on the book order page: www.mapmagnamund.com/id72.html). There are no copies of the fat edition left and my copy (which is still available at the time of writing) is the later, thin one. As I mentioned in my review of *The Buccaneers of Shadaki*, I have suffered at the hands of small presses on several occasions, but I had no problems whatsoever with my order, the price (£19.99) includes postage and packaging in the UK, and all copies purchased from Holmgard Press arrive with Dever's seal and signature.

The adventure begins in the early spring of MS 5102, seventeen years after the conclusion of *Lone Wolf 28: The Hunger of Sejanoz* (a conceit that neatly encapsulates the delay between planned and actual publication), which is not a problem for my Kai Grandmaster, True Friend, who only ages one year for every five (albeit at the cost of a silly name). The volume has a unique addition for a Lone Wolf collector's edition, a "Timeline of notable events in

Magnamund", which covers the interim since True
Friend put paid to the Autarch Sejanoz. In summary:
various hordes of evil minions have been sallying forth
from such fell places as the Doomlands of Naaros,
Kraknalorg Chasm, and the Chasm of Gorgoron; the
god Kai appeared before Lone Wolf to (somewhat
belatedly in my opinion) warn him that Naar is up to
his evil tricks again, following which – in MS 5101 – the
Grand Brumalmarc of the Icelands and his ice demon
allies attempted to invade the homeland of
Sommerlund and seismic disturbances opened a
gigantic chasm in the Darklands that extended the
dreaded Maakengorge. Magnamund is, it seems,
literally being rocked, and subterranean denizens that
should never see the light of day are pouring onto its
surface.

   True Friend has spent most of the above years
quietly, supervising the construction of the new Kai
Monastery on the Isle of Lorn and taking command
when Lone Wolf has been absent. The adventure
begins with Lone Wolf returning to the monastery to
hold a council, where he reveals that Magnamund is
indeed under a coordinated attack by an unknown
force. There are six armies attacking six different
locations and the top six ranking Kai Grandmasters are
despatched accordingly. Following True Friend's
slaying of Sejanoz, Chai rallied the New Kingdom
armies to inflict a decisive defeat on Bhanar, but after
more than a decade of peace, a Nadziranim sorcerer
named Bakhasa (who has a nasty habit of raising the
dead as unpleasant versions of their former cheery
selves) has seized the remote Bhanarian city of
Bakhasa. Zashnor is now in command of an Agarashi
horde from the Doomlands and appears to have
constructed a new Claw of Naar in an attempt to
succeed where Sejanoz failed, in invading Chai. True
Friend's mission is to recover the Eye of Agarash from

the new Khea-Khan before Zashnor can retrieve it and create a weapon of mass destruction by joining it with the replica Claw. The action begins with an airborne deployment to Chai and True Friend must race against the invading army to reach Pensei, the capital. The bulk of both the action and the story involve a prolonged but nonetheless exciting flight across Chai, from Pensei to Valus. The traditional combat finale of the first twenty-eight books has been replaced by a trio of final combats: first, Klüz, the Doomgah leader; then Xaol the Necromancer, raised from the dead since True Friend last killed him in *Lone Wolf 25: Trail of the Wolf*; and finally, Zashnor himself – along with his Zlanbeast. Each of these is a tough combat and there is little opportunity to rest between them, which brings me to my only criticism of a gamebook that otherwise meets all seventeen years' worth of expectations.

This is a *very* hard game to play and the difficulty is purely attritional: first, Zashnor has amassed a formidable army that is already rampaging around Chai when True Friend arrives in-country; second, once True Friend has the Eye of Agarash it exerts a long-term draining effect that pops up when least expected; third, in my gameplay there was only one opportunity for all of True Friend's endurance points to be restored and that relatively early on; finally, in my gameplay there were two occasions when two or more items of precious equipment were lost without the opportunity to recover or replace them. All of which to say that I think that *The Storms of Chai* would be nigh impossible to survive out of order – i.e., without True Friend having reached the rank of Sun Thane (level thirty-two out of a maximum of thirty-six) – and, for that matter, without the Grandmaster skills of both Deliverance and Weaponmastery. The volunteers at Project Aon have, amongst their many other services to Lone Wolf fans worldwide, helpfully provided a flow chart of each of the first twenty-eight books and although I suspect that the narrative of book 29 is no more linear than any of the others, the constant fighting against powerful enemies of all sorts makes it feel like what would be called a "hack and slash" dungeon crawl in *Dungeons & Dragons*. Certainly, this is one of the gamebooks where brawn (and luck) counts more than brains, although it is an entirely gripping hack and slash. The story ends with two unanswered questions: first, how did Zashnor get hold of the real Claw of Naar, which was supposed to be safe in Dessi? Second, who or what is the power behind the new assault on Magnamund? The first is revealed in the bonus adventure; the second will, one hopes, be at least partially answered in *Lone Wolf 30: Dead in the Deep*. The bonus adventure is "The Tides of Gorgoron" (written by Dever and Vincent Lazarri), where the reader adopts the persona of Lord Elkamo Doko, a Vakeros warrior-mage, a group of warriors who have been taught some of the skills of magic by the Elder Magi of Dessi. Lord Doko begins as second-in-command of a force sent to defend the Colo Bridge from the advancing Agarashi. The adventure is very entertaining, has a direct link to the narrative of *The Storms of Chai*, and the warrior-mage player character is perfectly-pitched – neither too similar nor too dissimilar to a Kai Grandmaster, thus making a perfect complement.

With book 29 selling so well, Dever has announced his future publishing plans as follows (the information is from a post of his on Facebook). Book 30 is due for release in December this year, book 31 in 2017, and book 32 – which completes the original series conception – in 2018. Parallel to the publication of books 30 to 32, Dever also intends to complete the job begun by Mongoose and continued by Mantikore

Verlag, publishing the collector's editions of books 23
to 28. The Holmgard Press edition of *The Hunger of
Sejanoz* will be particularly welcome, as it will contain
the usual three hundred and fifty gameplay sections
rather than the abridged three hundred that were for
reasons unknown published by Red Fox. Finally, Dever
has a five-year plan to re-release all the collector's
editions of books 1 to 22 as Holmgard Press imprints
so that by 2021 the entire series will be available in
Holmgard Press collector's editions. I wonder if this
last isn't a step too far? The final three books are likely
to sell out on pre-order like *The Storms of Chai* and
books 24 to 28 are only available at ludicrous prices on
the second-hand market (if at all), but the same is not
true of the previous books. Most long-term fans like
me will already have all of books 1 to 20 and some of
books 21 to 28, with some or all of the collector's
editions from 1 to 22. Dever surely doesn't expect
someone with all the 1 to 22 paperbacks and all the 1 to
22 collector's editions to buy the Holmgard Press
collector's editions as well? I can only hope that the
five-year plan reflects Dever's anticipation of a new,
younger generation of readers for the series rather
than hubris. And while I would love to see Lone Wolf
return to the popularity it enjoyed in the eighties, it
seems to me that the gamebook has become a very
niche market with the rapid advances in information
and communications technology at the end of the
twentieth century – the very reason the series was
dropped by Red Fox in 1998 (and for the seventeen-
year wait). I may seem very sceptical for such a die-
hard fan, but the problems the series has had over the
last thirty years have not exactly predisposed me
towards optimism. All of which to say, I wish Dever
the best of luck and will feel a lot more confident
about Holmgard Press when I hear that *Dead in the
Deep* has been published to schedule. Expect a TQF

review early next year... but don't hold your breath.
Rafe McGregor

Shadow Moths, by Cate Gardner (Frightful Horrors)

This little collection of two stories by Cate Gardner is the first in a planned line of ebooks from a new digital-only micro-press, Frightful Horrors. Its short length is reflected in its price (and it is available in the Kindle lending library and Kindle Unlimited to the respective subscribers). "We Make Our Own Monsters Here" follows Check Harding on his pilgrimage to the United Kingdom's best puppeteer, in hope of being his apprentice. On the way he checks into the peculiar Palmerston Hotel, where guests are provided with ladders to reach the light switches. "Blood Moth Kiss" is about Nola, who lives on a Royal Air Force base with partner Pete during a time of war. While he seems to go on missions, she is apparently beset by intangible exploding moths as atrocities loom. The book's description describes the author as an "award-nominated genre author", without specifying which genre that is – perhaps that's appropriate given that neither story falls neatly into any category. They're not westerns, that much is clear, but one could identify elements of fantasy, horror, sf and literary fiction in both, plus a dash of doomed, gothic romance in the second. Both are good. On my Kindle an unnecessary line of blank space appears after every paragraph, but in such a quick read that doesn't have time to become the mind-frazzling irritation it can be in a long novel.
Stephen Theaker ★★★☆☆

Stay Crazy, by Erika L. Satifka (Apex Publications)

Emmeline Kalberg, Em for short, is a nineteen-year-old young woman with mental health issues that landed her in a psychiatric hospital a while back. She doesn't remember quite what happened, but she's out and living with her mum and younger sister, and hoping to return to college when she's well enough. For now, though, her mum has set her up with a job at a big chain supermarket, Savertown USA, so that she doesn't spend too much time cooped up at home. The problem is, once she starts working there, she starts hearing voices. She's used to that, given that "even alone in her room, drifting off to sleep, Em always kept her music on low, a ward to keep the voices at bay", but the voice in the supermarket is more persistent than usual, talks to her through the ID chips in the products, and doesn't follow her home. It warns about bad stuff happening, and as supermarket colleagues begin to meet bad ends she starts to take it seriously. As the situation worsens, the reader can't be sure what's really going on, but we do know that Em is experiencing *something*, and we're stuck on the sidelines hoping that one way or another she makes it through. It's a short, direct novel, and one described by some readers as comedic, although for me its portrayal of mental illness seemed too tragically realistic to be all that funny. Its depiction of life working in a supermarket is also spot on, showing very accurately the justifiable pride people take in their hard work, the rivalries between departments, and the expectation that employees will be excited about visits from upper management. As someone who only rarely made it to the dizzy heights of shelf-stacker in my brief supermarket career, I was impressed and convinced by how quickly Em took to it. Comparisons have been made to Philip K. Dick, and there are definite similarities with books like *Valis* and *Radio Free Albemuth*, one difference being that Dick's books uncovered what was *really* happening, while *Stay Crazy* leaves everything open to doubt. I was reminded too of Maria Bamford's Netflix show *Lady Dynamite*, which also shows a woman leaving a psychiatric

hospital and returning to a world that seems as crazy as she ever was. People who like one may well enjoy the other. *Stephen Theaker* ★★★☆☆

Comics

Captain Midnight, Vol. 1: On the Run, by Joshua Williamson, Fernando Dagnino and chums (Dark Horse Books)

I loved Chuck Dixon's *Airboy* series from the eighties, so this book's similar mix of superplanes and superheroics really appealed to me. Captain Midnight was a hero back in World War II, who fought the Nazis with his engineering genius, two strong fists, a suit that didn't let him fly but did let him glide, and his allies, the Secret Squadron. They kept going after  he went missing, but now, decades later, he's back, flying out of a storm in the Bermuda Triangle to land on the *U.S.S. Ronald Reagan*. The authorities are suspicious, his friends are all elderly, and his enemies are still up to no good. This first volume only collects four issues, but it's a good introduction to the character. We get to see what he's about, what keeps him going, and why we'd be interested in reading more about him. His return to action after a long absence obviously has strong echoes of Captain America, and fans of *Tom Strong* and *Miracleman* might also notice some similarities, but it feels fresh and fun, not least in the way Captain Midnight swoops and soars. Like Batroc with his leaping, or going up and down the half-pipe in a Tony Hawks game, there's a joy in the sheer physics of it. *Stephen Theaker* ★★★☆☆

Ms. Marvel Vol. 1: No Normal, by G. Willow Wilson and Adrian Alphona (Marvel)

Kamala Khan is a smart fifteen-year-old girl, living in New Jersey with loving parents who quite understandably don't want her going out at night and an older brother who's keener on virtue than finding a job. She works hard at school, has a pair of good friends, clever Bruno and proud Nakiyi, and somehow deals with the microaggressions of popular white girls without losing her temper. Her hero is Captain Marvel; Kamala's been known to write quite popular fanfiction where the Avengers protect the My Little Ponies. One night she gets fed up with her parents and sneaks out to what turns out to be a rather crummy party. Nothing bad happens till she is on her way home: the terrigen mists descend, and she wakes up in a black shell, transformed into a younger Captain Marvel. It looks like Kamala is an Inhuman, with shape-changing powers that she'll explore in a bunch of different ways over the rest of the book. Growing a big hand, looking like a shop window dummy, shrinking to the size of a mouse – she'll get the hang of it all while amusing the reader and trying to extricate Bruno's idiot brother from a tight spot. Like the young Peter Parker, she's a teenage superhero trying to do the right thing despite the pressures and obligations of school, family and friends, and this feels from the off like classic Marvel at its best: contemporary, imaginative, funny and relevant, with excellent artwork. Kamala is an utterly charming fangirl hero, tailor-made for modern teenagers. *Stephen Theaker* ★★★★☆

Savage Dragon Archives, Volume One, by Erik Larsen (Image Comics)

This huge black and white collection includes issues one to three of the original Savage Dragon mini-series, plus the first twenty-one issues of the ongoing series, all of it written and drawn by the character's creator, Erik Larsen. As with the Walking Dead books, there is nothing to indicate where one issue begins and the next ends, making for an intense helter-skelter of a reading experience, fights with full-page villains constantly bursting out of nowhere. There are moments of peace here and there, but the Dragon's life is not one of quiet contemplation. He was found in a vacant burning lot, his skin green and tough, his head sporting a fin, and his arms as thick as tree-trunks. He remembers nothing about his life, but remembers baseball and the president. A desperate friend, Frank, finds a way to finagle the Dragon into joining the police force (in a way that he'll come to greatly regret), and thus begins the jolly green giant's career as the

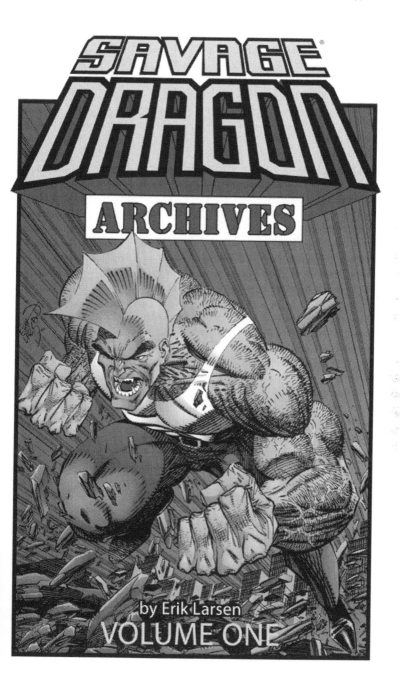

official strong arm of the law. It's tremendously exciting, bonkers, and inventive, one bizarre battle following another, with very little time wasted on introducing the villains – they just get on with it – and the ongoing storylines and mysteries are always ticking away nicely. The artwork to me seems quite similar to John Byrne's (ironically, since he comes in for some stick in the book as Johnny Redbeard), with the drama of Frank Miller, and the crackling kinetic energy of Jack Kirby. Reading it in colour might have helped me to make visual sense of some fight scenes quicker, but it still looked really nice in black and white. It reminded me of what I like so much about *Invincible*, a much later hit from the same publisher, in that it feels like a whole superhero universe in one book – even the guest appearances from Spawn and the Teenage Mutant Ninja Turtles are made to feel like an organic part of the over-the-top storytelling. Is it truly good? Hard to judge, because it's playing by its own mad logic, but it's certainly an enjoyable and unique experience. The subsequent five volumes were, on the whole, just as enjoyable. *Stephen Theaker* ★★★★☆

Films

Don't Breathe, by Fede Alvarez and Rodo Sayagues (Screen Gems et al.)

So tense it doesn't need a true protagonist.

Don't Breathe, a turn-the-tables tale about three burglars who become their blind victim's prey, offers no superb dialogue, no complicated internal struggles, and no computer-generated imagery-heavy superhero battles.

So what's with all the glowing reviews from critics and audience members alike? It all comes down to the

one thing that the film, directed by Fede Alvarez, delivers masterfully and relentlessly: tension.

The tenseness starts immediately with an aerial view of a seemingly vacant street bordered by houses. Unsettling music plays as the camera slowly zooms in on something disturbing happening in the middle of that street. The tone is set, and that tone will remain until the end.

Rocky (Jane Levy), the closest thing *Don't Breathe* has to a protagonist, lives in a dilapidated Detroit neighborhood with her poverty-stricken mother and her younger sister. She wants to get enough money to whisk away her sister to California. The problem is how Rocky makes her money: by burgling wealthy people's homes with her impulsive boyfriend Money (Daniel Zovatto) and their quiet accomplice Alex (Dylan Minnette), who has an obvious crush on Rocky. When Money gets tipped off about a big score at the blind man's house, Rocky's dream is within grasp.

As the group explores the home, floorboards creak, characters whisper, and the camera lingers on potential weapons like tools on a pegboard or a gun under a bed. The rest of the film offers, if you'll pardon the expression, a blindingly vast array of twists, narrow escapes, violent beatings, claustrophobic encounters, and, most nerve-wracking, characters' attempts to stifle their own cries of pain or fear in the presence of the blind man.

Early in the film, Money says, "Just because he's blind, don't mean he's a fuckin' saint." That assessment, albeit crude, turns out to be right on the money. Sorry.

The antagonist, played by Stephen Lang and known only as "the blind man", may be older, but he's no Mr. Magoo. He's a Gulf War vet who got a bad lot in life: first he lost his sight in battle, then he lost his daughter to a car accident. With his ripped arms and his hulking Rottweiler, the blind man is an imposing fellow. He tosses people around like rag dolls, repeatedly punches them in the face, and doesn't hesitate when it comes to pulling the trigger. He is brutish and unrelenting.

The title *Don't Breathe* serves as a warning to the characters in the film, but it's also a warning to *you*, the viewer, who becomes an accomplice by indirectly participating in this crime of a disabled vet. There are several severely tense scenes with no music and no sound during which the characters strive to remain silent... to not even breathe. And you, too, don't want to breathe. *Douglas J. Ogurek* ★★★★★

Ghostbusters: Answer the Call, by Katie Dippold and Paul Feig (Columbia Pictures et al.)

There's déjà vu in the neighbourhood.

Ivan Reitman, speaking of the development of the original *Ghostbusters* film,[1] recalls Dan Aykroyd's first treatment as featuring many groups of futuristic ghostbusters and about fifty large-scale monsters (of which the marshmallow man was just one), with an estimated production cost of (only half-jokingly) $300 million. This is not the movie that ended up being made in 1984; nor, sadly, is it the film that rebooted in 2016.

Ghostbusters: Answer the Call is by no means a bad production (objectively, it's better than *Ghostbusters II*), but it's the *same* as the original: neither reboot nor remake but rather a shadow; a "based on" in much the same way that *Blues Brothers 2000* changed the details but followed exactly the same blueprint as *The Blues Brothers*. Not unlike covering a song that was near-perfect to begin with, the results of such mimicry can only be disappointing. It's nobody's fault. If not for nostalgia tipping the scales the lead cast (all women, all comedians) would near enough match up to that of the original movie. Likewise much of the dialogue, which is funny and well-delivered, just not as etched-in-stone memorable as those *bon mots* that have been quoted so often these last thirty-plus years. Chris Hemsworth differs from Rick Moranis in the quirkiness of his supporting role. Karan Soni brings something as the takeaway delivery man. But really, what else is there to talk about?

Yes, there are cameos, but these are mostly counterproductive. The bust of Harold Ramis brings home the sad truth that he's no longer with us. Bill Murray's appearance leaves us to question his refusal to be involved in countless other proposed *Ghostbusters* projects. Dan Aykroyd shows that he could easily still have answered the call. Ernie Hudson comes in late – still the token fourth member – while the less said about Sigourney Weaver's effort the better. Only Moranis had the good sense not to return, which is how it should be. If continuity is to be thrown out (which after all is the liberty afforded by a reboot) then what value the cameo except to assuage the misgivings of old-time fans, yet in the process stirring their unfulfilled hunger for past glories? Even the brief snatch of Ray Parker Jnr's classic *Ghostbusters* song isn't so much paying homage as twisting the knife.

When the big scary evil comes to its flaccid end, *Ghostbusters: Answer the Call* is neither here nor there, nor anywhere else for that matter: not a shot-for-shot remake; not a sequel; and – let's be honest – not really much of a reboot. By all means cast Melissa McCarthy, Kristen Wiig, Kate McKinnon and Leslie Jones. They're very good, so why not? But pour some juice into the script! Cross the streams and go for something new, not merely: "Who you gonna call? Er, 1984." Wake up, Hollywood: three decades later, the future is here; so why not go *further* into the future?

Why not reboot from Dan Aykroyd's at-the-time unrealisable first concept and have several competing ghostbusting groups and a threat that's been in some way escalated, if only by inflation?

With a blank slate *Ghostbusters: Answer the Call* could have been anything. It could have been just as good as its classic forerunner, perhaps even (and here's

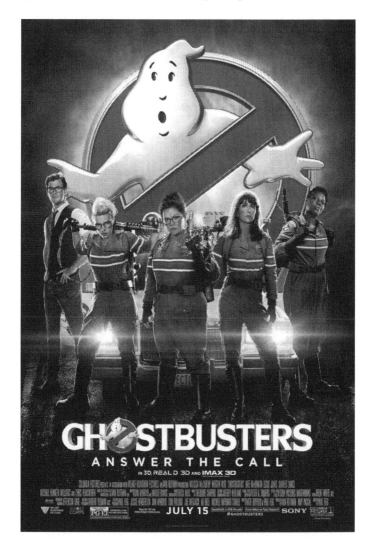

a thought the writers, producers and director seem not to have considered) better. Instead, we got more of the same: merely ripples of reprise. We got half-heartedly slimed. Again. *Jacob Edwards*

---

1. Audio commentary, 12:10-12:30.

Ouija: Origin of Evil, by Mike Flanagan and Jeff Howard (Allspark Pictures et al.)

Will this prequel overcome its predecessor's mediocrity? Yes.

This Halloween season, horror film fans had slim pickings at the theatre. And I wouldn't be surprised if, like me, they felt disappointed when they learned about the season's feature offering: *Ouija: Origin of Evil*.

Last year, *Ouija* had a few scares, but overall, it wasn't memorable. Thus, one would think that when filmmakers questioned whether they should do another one, surely the planchette would slide to "no". But that wasn't the case. A new writer/director (Mike Flanagan) and co-writer (Jeff Howard) came on board – pun intended – and, surprisingly, they pulled off a much better film.

Ouija: Origin of Evil doesn't offer much that the horror aficionado hasn't seen before. However, this story of a Hasbro classic gone haywire effectively uses the tools at its disposal, offering an intimate and creepy take, replete with nerve-wracking scenes and jump scares, on how the game wreaks havoc on a small family living in 1960s Los Angeles.

Alice Zander and daughters Lina and Doris use rigged séances not so much as a money-making scheme, but rather as a means of bringing solace to those who've lost loved ones. Then they add a Ouija board to spice up their routine. Things get dicey when

a spirit starts communicating with youngest daughter Doris via the board. Is it deceased husband/father Roger, or is it something more malicious? Father Tom Hogan, the priest/headmaster at the girls' school, gets involved and the spiritual threat intensifies.

The Ouija rules are simple: 1) never play alone; 2) never play in a graveyard; and 3) always say goodbye. But if you're going to show rules in a movie, you better break them! And *Ouija: Origin of Evil* does.

The characters in *Ouija: Origin of Evil* are more fully developed than those in *Ouija*. Widow Alice struggles to make ends meet, yet she genuinely wants to use her machinations to help people. She even declines payment from a client who nearly has a heart attack. Teenager Lina is bright and well-behaved, but her interest in classmate Mikey gets jeopardised by all the spiritual mischief going on. Yet it's young Doris, bullied by her classmates, who undergoes the biggest change under the spell of the spirits. Watch for a particularly satisfying scene in which one of Doris's tormentors gets a taste of his own medicine. In another scene, Doris asks Mikey if he wants "to hear something cool", then proceeds to describe in intricate detail what it feels like to be strangled.

Flanagan and company use several techniques to jiggle the nerves. For instance, when the camera lingers on ordinary objects, one cringes with uncertainty: will something pop onto the screen? In the opening scene, the only sound that fills the séance parlour is that of the clock. Done before, but still effective.

Still, nothing jacks up the heart rate more than when a character peers through the planchette's glass opening, which helps identify any spiritual entities that might be present. As the panning camera shows a warped view of a room, there's always the chance that something will appear. It's intense!

The fear potency gets stronger with a host of other horror film tricks: ceiling walking, wall crawling, milky eyes, impossible facial contortions, and getting yanked around by unseen entities.

Ouija: Origin of Evil may not have broken new ground in the horror genre, but it did entertain consistently. In an age of *Candy Crush Saga*, *Minecraft*, and other smartphone games, it's refreshing to see people come together around a board game-inspired film for some good old-fashioned scares. *Douglas J. Ogurek* ★★★★☆

Suicide Squad, by David Ayer (Atlas Entertainment et al.)

Popsicles and lollipops advertised, mostly stale bread delivered.

The playful colours and reckless tone of *Suicide Squad* advertisements suggest a departure from the typical superhero film. Unfortunately, excepting the antics of one flamboyant couple, the film is too dull and safe to live up to the hype.

Director David Ayers presents a Gotham where one of the most beloved superheroes appears to be dead. The ruthless Dr Amanda Waller (Viola Davis) assembles the worst of the worst criminals as a safety measure. *Suicide Squad* starts strong, giving viewers a taste of the "metahuman" recruits' powers, ranging from Deadshot's (Will Smith) incredible accuracy to the pyrokinesis of remorseful gangster Diablo (Jay Hernandez).

The antiheroes get microchips embedded in their necks – they misbehave, and boom! – then soldier Rick Flag leads them on a mission to rescue an unknown operative. In the meantime, archaeologist Dr June Moone (also Flag's girlfriend) struggles to subdue Enchantress, the ancient witch who resides within her.

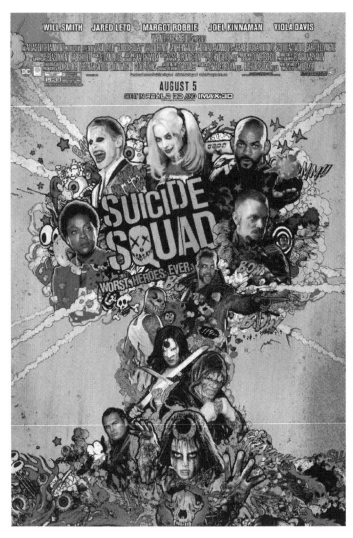

Moon fails, so the Enchantress sets in motion a plan to destroy the world.

The squad blasts and pounds away at Enchantress's faceless, lumpy-skinned henchmen that an eight-year-old girl could defeat. Half of the squad consists of underdeveloped dullards with little to no backstory. For instance, Australian burglar Boomerang adds nothing to the film and swordswoman Katana seems to spend more time posing than fighting. Winning the booby prize for most annoying character, however, is Killer Croc. This sewer-dwelling goon makes comments that make you want to slap your forehead.

Enchantress spends too much time using her magic to swirl garbage in the sky to build a "machine" that will destroy humanity, while her brother, a flaming monster with elastic burning body parts, protects her. How long does it take to build this thing? Also, one has to question why Enchantress, arguably more powerful than any of the Suicide Squad members, would resort to hand-to-hand combat.

An Adorably Idiosyncratic Couple
What makes this film worth seeing is the eccentric duo of the Joker (not a Suicide Squad member) and Harley Quinn. Their effervescent personalities and their vivid costumes echo the vitality of the film's soundtrack, which ranges from Eminem and Kanye West to Ozzy Osbourne and The Rolling Stones.

Jared Leto's Joker admirably fills the shoes of Jack Nicholson and Heath Ledger, but also puts a new spin on the beloved arch villain. This bling- and tattoo-laden Joker retains Ledger's dramatic gestures and adds a penchant for baring silver-capped teeth in the style of James Bond's Jaws.

Then there is Dr Harleen Quinzel (Margot Robbie), who the Joker seduced, then transformed into quirky criminal Harley Quinn. Quinn stands out by far as the Suicide Squad's most entertaining character. "Huh? What was that? I should kill everyone and escape?" she says in her Brooklyn accent before an audience of simultaneously attracted and wary law enforcers. "Sorry. The voices. Ahaha, I'm kidding! Jeez! That's not what they really said."

Quinn fills a gap in the world of female superheroes.

The bubble blowing, the exaggerated swagger, and the cutesy Betty Boopesque sexuality merge with the questionable insanity, plus Quinn is somewhat of a sweetheart. She wields a baseball bat that says "Good Night". Her necklace – it's more like a dog collar – that says "PUDDIN" (her nickname for the Joker) in bold gold letters reveals her obsession with the villain.

Suicide Squad offers a couple of iconic raised shots featuring these two. In one, weapons and dolls surround the Joker, who lies on the floor and laughs distinctively. In another, the lovers kiss in a vat of unknown liquid – is that pudding? – surrounded by swirls of the Joker's colourful paint.

"Would you die for me?" asks the Joker. "No, no, no. That's too easy. Would you live for me?"

Don't be surprised to find yourself rooting not so much for the Suicide Squad to succeed, but rather for the Joker and Harley Quinn to reunite. Interesting, isn't it, that the most entertaining characters in this film really don't have any super powers? A testimony to the magic of character.

Alas, despite the vibrancy of these two, Suicide Squad doesn't make the cut when compared to this year's other superb superhero films like *Captain America: Civil War*, *X-Men: Apocalypse*, and especially *Deadpool. Douglas J. Ogurek* ★★★☆☆

Television

Preacher, Season 1, by Seth Rogen, Evan Goldberg and chums (Amazon Prime Video)

The comic *Preacher* was in development for so long, first as a film and then as a television series, that you might easily have concluded that there was something fundamentally unfilmable about the project. You –

FROM THE MINDS BEHIND
BREAKING BAD, *THE FAST AND THE FURIOUS* AND *THIS IS THE END*

THE BEGINNING IS NIGH

PREACHER
5.22 SUN 10|9c amc

okay, I – might have thought there was no way this programme, having finally made it to the screen, could possibly live up to the standards of the comic. And it's quite an old comic now. Would it still work? Well, anyone who had those thoughts, me included, has been proven utterly wrong by a programme that rollicked with an energy rarely seen on television, that has left every other programme since feeling muted and low-key. But not everyone has read the comic, and the show is not quite the same as the comic, so I should say something about the story. Jesse Custer (Dominic Cooper) is a half-assed preacher in a dirty, rotten town. His church helper Emily (played by Lucy Griffiths, the former Maid Marian in the BBC's *Robin Hood*) has a crush on him, but he's in no fit state to notice. Then three lightning bolts strike his life. Genesis, the offspring of an angel and a demon, embeds itself within his body, giving him the power to command. The vampire Cassidy (Joseph Gilgun) drops out of an aeroplane and pals up with Jesse in a bar. And old flame Tulip O'Hare (Ruth Negga) roars back into town, wanting Jesse to help her get revenge on an old colleague who left them in the wind. All of a sudden Jesse's in the middle of a lot of trouble, so it's a good thing he is surprisingly handy in a fight. It seems as if this show might, like *The Walking Dead*, cluster its seasons around particular locations, as this one is mainly set in the town of Annville, but it works very well, and at the end of a very satisfying season it's a treat to know how much more from the comics is still in store. The cast is brilliant, coping with the shifts in tone from horror to comedy as if it was all the same thing, and without exception perfectly portraying the characters we've loved and loathed from the comics. Credit to Jeanie Bacharach, casting director, who must have clapped herself on the back for a job well done after watching each episode. One minute it reminds you of *Justified* or *Fargo*, the next it's *Monty Python* or *Hitch-Hiker's Guide to the Galaxy*, all while successfully reclaiming its storylines from *Supernatural* in a way that *Constantine* didn't quite manage. Altogether it adds up to something totally new. Confident, brash and bloody, I reckon it's my favourite programme on television right now. *Stephen Theaker* ★★★★★

The X-Files, Season 10, by Chris Carter and chums (Ten Thirteen Productions et al.)

It took me a little while to warm up to *The X-Files* when it first began. Round about the episode "Deep Throat" is where I started to become a fan, rather than someone who watched it because my girlfriend was watching it. Before then I had a big problem with the way Mulder would throw lots of so-called evidence at Scully in support of his irrational crackpot theories, evidence that in our world had been totally discredited, and then be proven right by what came next. That led to a resurgent real-world interest in the paranormal, just before mobile phones and their cameras laid ghosts, nessies and bigfeet to rest forever, but I made my peace with it after realising that on Mulder's Earth there is good evidence, because in his world monsters and aliens do exist. Of course I then became frustrated with the idea of Scully being the rational, scientific one, when she ignores all the evidence – the implication being that in our world that's what our scientists do with regard to the paranormal. This new season, following hard on the heels of Gillian Anderson and David Duchovny's showstopping performances in shows like *Hannibal* and *Californication*, severely tested the grudging peace I had made with all that. A two-part story, "My Struggle", where the worst nightmares of anti-vaxxers and rightwing talk show hosts come true, for example,

left me very cold, to the extent that I'd call it irresponsible. If it had been good dramatically and creatively, that would have been one thing, but it was like a Syfy original movie written by the kind of people you block on Twitter. Similarly, "Babylon" explores the aftermath of an apparent terrorist bombing, and you wait for the supernatural twist, for our stereotyped assumptions to be undercut... and it doesn't come. The paranormal element is that Mulder is apparently now able to enter people's minds, *Dreamscape*-style, if he takes the right drugs. And don't get me started on the "everything you know is a lie" bit they try to pull, yet again. Those were three of the worst episodes of the programme to date. But I'm still glad it's back. I'd rather have Mulder and Scully back for bad episodes than none at all – and the three other episodes of this short series were good enough to outweigh the bad. "Founder's Mutation" and "Home Again" both delivered a series of good scares, while "Mulder & Scully Meet the Were-Monster", featuring the hilarious Rhys Darby as a man who turns into a lizard creature, or so it seems, was a delight from start to finish, one of my favourite ever episodes. So a mixed season, but that's how it often was with *The X-Files*, and even the bad episodes had their share of startlingly weird imagery. What worked, worked very well. I hope there are more seasons to come. *Stephen Theaker* ★★★☆☆

Notes

Also Received, But Not Yet Reviewed
Notes by Stephen Theaker

*   Baxter, Stephen, *The Massacre of Mankind* (Orion): an authorised sequel to *The War of the Worlds*.

- Drake, Darrell, *A Star-Reckoner's Lot* (self-published): a "treacherous journey through Iranian legends and ancient history".
- Edgington, Ian, and D'Israeli, *Scarlet Traces, Volume One* (2000AD): another *War of the Worlds* sequel, in comics form this time. Unusually, this is a creator-owned property that *2000 AD* has bought outright.
- Egan, Greg, *The Four Thousand, the Eight Hundred* (Subterranean Press)
- Eggleton, Robert, *Rarity from the Hollow* (Dog Horn Publishing)
- Hicks, Faith Erin, *The Stone Heart* (First Second): a graphic novel.
- Lowder, Christopher, Gerry Finlay-Day, Dave Gibbons and chums, *Dan Dare: The 2000 AD Years, Vol. 2* (2000 AD): the second and final collection of the adventures of the rufty-tufty version of Dan Dare.
- Maberry, Jonathan (ed.), *Out of Tune, Book II* (Journalstone Publishing): a themed anthology of stories inspired by classic folk songs.
- Parent, Jason, *Wrathbone and Other Stories* (Comet Press): five stories "with a *Tales from the Crypt* vibe".
- Salmonson, Jessica Amanda, *The Complete Weird Epistles of Penelope Pettiweather, Ghost Hunter* (The Alchemy Press)
- Smith, Alex, *Hive* (Muzzleland Press): from a TQF contributor!
- Wilson, Kai Ashante, *A Taste of Honey* (Tor.com): this was great. Review next issue.

About TQF

Copyright

ISBN (print): 978-1-910387-19-1
ISBN (epub): 978-1-910387-20-7

ISSN (print): 1747-6083
ISSN (online): 1747-6075

Website: www.theakersquarterly.blogspot.com

Email: theakersquarterlyfiction@gmail.com

Lulu Store: www.lulu.com/silveragebooks

Feedbooks: www.feedbooks.com/userbooks/tag/tqf

Submissions: Submissions are very welcome! See website for guidelines and terms and reading periods.

Advertising: We welcome ad swaps with small press publishers and other creative types, and we'll run ads for relevant new projects from former contributors.

Sending material for review: We are happy to look at anything that's fantasy-related. We prefer to receive books for review in epub or mobi format, and comics in pdf. Feel free to send ebooks without querying first, but it's fair to warn you that we've only reviewed about 15% of items received since 2011, and even then that's often been stuff we've actively requested from places like NetGalley. In this issue, 14 items reviewed were paid for by the reviewers, one was supplied via Audible, and one was supplied by the publisher.

Mission statement: The primary goal of *Theaker's Quarterly Fiction* is to keep going. If you're wondering why we do something a particular way, our primary goal is probably why.

Copyright and legal: All works are copyright the respective authors, who have assumed all responsibility for any legal problems arising from publication of their material. Other material copyright Stephen Theaker and John Greenwood.

Published in Theaker's Paperback Library during December 2016.

Other Publications

Theaker's Quarterly Fiction #9–54, 56
Stephen Theaker and John Greenwood (eds)

Theaker's Quarterly Fiction #55
Howard Watts (ed.)

Theaker's Quarterly Fiction #1–8
Stephen Theaker (ed.)

Space University Trent: Hyperparasite
Walt Brunston

There Are Now a Billion Flowers
The Hatchling (forthcoming)
John Greenwood

The Mercury Annual
Pilgrims at the White Horizon
Michael Wyndham Thomas

The Conan Doyle Weirdbook
Rafe McGregor (ed.)

Professor Challenger in Space
Quiet, the Tin Can Brains Are Hunting!
The Fear Man
His Nerves Extruded

The Doom That Came to Sea Base Delta
The Day the Moon Wept Blood
Stephen Theaker

Five Forgotten Stories
John Hall

Elephant
Harsh Grewal

Elsewhere
Steven Gilligan

New Words #1–4
John Greenwood, Steven Gilligan
and Stephen Theaker (eds)

Forthcoming Attractions

Expect **Theaker's Quarterly Fiction #58** later this month. We will re-open to submissions in January.

Our blog can be read here:
www.theakersquarterly.blogspot.com

Stephen tweets every few days or so at:
www.twitter.com/Rolnikov

The zine has its own Twitter account too:
www.twitter.com/TheakersQrtly

Our email address is:
theakersquarterlyfiction@gmail.com

Printed in Great Britain
by Amazon